LOUISA REID

GLOVES OFF

**GUPPY
BOOKS**

GLOVES OFF
is a GUPPY BOOK

First published in the UK in 2019 by
Guppy Publishing Ltd,
Bracken Hill,
Cotswold Road,
Oxford OX2 9JG

Text © Louisa Reid, 2019

978 1 913101 00 8

1 3 5 7 9 10 8 6 4 2

Papers used by Guppy Books are from well-managed forests and other responsible sources.

MIX
Paper from
responsible sources
FSC® C018072

GUPPY PUBLISHING LTD Reg. No. 11565833

A CIP catalogue record for this book is available from the British Library.

Typeset in Gill Sans and Garamond by Falcon Oast Graphic Art Ltd, www.falcon.uk.com
Printed and bound in Great Britain by Clays Ltd, Elcograf S.p.A

GLOVES OFF

www.guppybooks.co.uk

Also by Louisa Reid:

BLACK HEART BLUE

LIES LIKE LOVE

www.louisareid.com

*"Going in one more round
when you don't think you can.
That's what makes all the
difference in your life."*

— Rocky Balboa

ROADKILL

i taste the street —
it's filthy,
gritty and hard,
and it has

                                                   knocked

                   all the

                         breath

out of my body.

slammed low,
i grope for my bag,
stinging shame in my palms,
on my knees,
and my chin.

i don't get up.
i stare at the ground,

something in my eye.

RESCUE

waiting for the thunder of feet to fade,
for the taunts to be swallowed
by the blare and shout of traffic —

who finds me?
who scrapes me off the street
and helps me home?

(oh, god,
how long did i
lie
there?)

i don't like to be
SEEN.
and — like *that* —
SPOTTED
at my worst.
i like to pretend
that no one knows
who i am,
that i'm hiding well,
hiding here,
in front of you —

invisible,
nevertheless.

but when you're
        down and out,
                knocked
                        on the ground,
                                crumpled —

it's clear that someone put you there,
and that you didn't fight back.

too weak.

too wet.

even so,
i remember to say thank you
to the woman who drives me home.

manners cost nothing.

FOR SHE'S A JOLLY GOOD FELLOW

i turn my key in the door,
and hear mikey's voice –
"she's home, she's home! lily! lil!"
he runs towards me,
grabs my hand,
before i can escape upstairs,
and drags me into the sitting room
where mum and aunty clare are waiting
with balloons,
and a fountain of silly string explodes.

"happy birthday to you!"
they chorus
in voices so loud
the whole street will hear,
even the baby is bouncing
and cooing in time.

i crush the rest of the day inside my fist,
and smile.

SWEET SIXTEEN

there's birthday kisses and cake.
a tower of pink candles
flickers and flares,
mikey claps his hands,
jumps up and down –
our sofa his trampoline,
as i blow out my age – all sixteen at once –
and screw my eyes tight,
and make my wish.

"look what i got you!" mikey cries,
shoving a parcel into my hands,
and i peel back the tape,
peep inside,
"oh wow," i say, "oh, thanks, mikey, aunty clare, that's
great."
make-up,
– a palette of war paint.

"you can get married now," says aunty clare,
giving me a wink,
no ta
"or just play the lottery," she hands me a ticket,
for tomorrow night's draw,

and i smile at the thought.

mum's made me a scarf,
crocheted perfection, matching hat and gloves,
in rainbow hues,

> "do you like it, lil?"
> she asks, watching me,
> so anxiously,
> "it's getting colder now,
> they'll keep you warm."

i wrap myself in her love,
they're perfect, mum, so beautiful.

but i know i can never wear this stuff
anywhere near school.

DANCING QUEENS

mum cranks up Abba,
and mikey insists
that we play some games —
musical statues, he decides,

so we all join in,
and let him win.

"didn't you do a pass the parcel, aunty bern?"
mikey wonders,
and we laugh, tease mum,
then i grab my cousin and swing him
round
and round
until we fall on the sofa,
dizzy and daft,
and i tickle him until all I hear is his laugh.

BERNADETTE (1)

When you were born you were perfect.
And now,
Standing here,
Looking at you —
Sixteen! —
I watch you and wonder,
At the shape of your face,
The arch of your brow,
The bow of your lips,
The length of your neck,
The strength of your back,
The curve of your cheeks,
The joy of your laugh,
Your heart, so sweet.

Oh Lily,
You are my masterpiece.

WE ALL FALL DOWN

my dad thinks i'm clumsy.

i don't let him see
all the bruises —
sometimes, though, he'll look at me twice
and ask questions that make me
wince and hide.

"happy birthday, lil," he shouts down the phone,
the roar of a motorway
growling hello.

he's not home tonight.
he works long hours
far away
for not much pay,
which is why I need
to do well at school,
to find a way to rise above,
they say.

but what if you can't concentrate?
what if there's always too much noise?

sixteen –
should know what's what,
how to deal
with what i'm not.

i lie awake,
as sirens strafe the early hours –
someone else's problem,
but,
still,
close enough to remind us
no one's safe
round here.

3 A.M.

and the front door opens, shuts.
i can hear mum in the hallway,
murmuring, the sound of
lights being turned on,
and the kettle humming,
fridge sucking open, shut.

i wonder
if it's dad.

standing at the top of the stairs,
i listen in.

uncle ray.

oh, god.

go away.

"MORNING,"

he says, sitting there,
feet under the table,
cooked breakfast round his mouth,
mopping up yolk
with a piece of fried bread.
"all right? get the girl some grub, bern. lazy cow,"
he laughs,
eyeing me,
no card or present, that's no surprise.
mum steps to the cupboard,
her face grey and pouchy,
yawning behind her hand.

they've talked all night,
his voice echoed
up the stairs,
into my room,
vibrating, deep and low.
he likes the sound of it,
sings karaoke at the weekends,
when he can.

and now this morning
ray is brazen,
has shaved his face
with one of dad's razors.
"she never did pull her weight, eh, lil?"
he laughs at his joke, gestures at my mum,
but i don't smile
or sit down.

"come on then,"
he says to mum,
"get into gear.
get that arse moving, eh?"

ray comes over
when dad's away
and mum
lets him in.

if dad were here,
he'd tell ray to sling his hook.

once i saw mum open her purse
and hand over all she had.

i know his knock:
a hammer.
if no one answers
he calls through the letter box,
then comes round the back,
"i know you're in there,"
he shouts.

i'm a coward. i make her face him alone.

see you later, mum,
i kiss her goodbye
and slam the door behind me.

uncle ray is
in the police,
        you'd think
        that you could trust him.

BERNADETTE (2)

The past
Follows me,
A stalker
Who knows everything I've ever regretted,
Every shameful moment I can't forget.
My brother, Ray, grins.
His face is over the breakfast table
And
His fist is in my belly
In the alley
Near school
Twenty years ago,
Taking my bus money,
Pulling my hair,
Telling his friends they can have a ride.

And I'm still a kid
Who can't tell him where to go.

Every day
I watch my daughter leave,
See her walk away,

Close the door,
Everything on her shoulders.
And I try not to cry at the strength that somehow
she has learned.

What now for me?
I sit in her room and stare at the pictures on her
walls.
She'd hate to know I was here
Touching her things,
Trying to worm my way inside her thoughts.

I talk to Lil of how she'll leave all this
Behind,
And that thought is the saddest one of all.

SCREW SCHOOL (I)

it's all
that i can do to find my way to school,
my feet doing
everything i'd rather they didn't –
as if the compass points only one way.

avoiding the noise and bother of the bus,
the shoving and pushing and not enough room
knowing that i will sit alone,
i take the long route.

no one is waiting this morning.

i spend the day dodging
faces,
jeers.

later, homewards,
  i walk again
     down the
        autumn strewn streets,
           kicking leaves and litter,
            fighting fumes,
               looking over my shoulder,
pretending that i'm not so slow.

(if someone tries to get me
i'll freeze,
grabbed and caught,
my scream is already ready,
vice tight, a band across my chest
and i will hate that i can't run.)

there are peeping shadows everywhere.
i tell myself i see things that
are not there.

BERNADETTE (3)

Watching the clock.
Where are you?

When you were small
You were my tiny shadow
It was almost as if we breathed as one.

I knew what made you happy,
What made you sad.

When you were growing up
I'd tell your dad we'd had a lovely day
And it was true,
I suppose.
You never seemed to mind
Staying at home and playing in the yard.

We made mud pies in summer,
Splashed in the paddling pool,
Grew strawberries in pots
From seeds I ordered down a phone line,
Avoiding facing faces.

You and your dad brought home
Tadpoles from the park.
We made a makeshift pond and watched them grow,
You laughed as they
Changed,
Tried to catch
The baby frogs
When they jumped.

When you started school
I didn't show you how to make friends
And keep them,
To make connections
Or make your mark.
I didn't show you how to walk in steps as bold
And bright as your smile,
Or that your heart could burn
With all the dreams it dared.

ANOTHER DAY DONE

i wander home,

and follow the road as
        far as it will go.
i watch the sky
        and think that if i could only run
                i might catch the disappearing sun,
                        snatch the
                                light,
                                        hitch a ride
out of here, to the other place,
another world where i am
someone
new.

i tried it once,
        chasing fast as i could go,
                panting
                        stumbling,
                                tripping over uneven stones,
down the lane, towards the
wasteland,
metal scarred,
that runs behind the houses to

a place that isn't a place any more.

surely there, i'd find it –
        a pool of gold.
                but the sun
                        outran me.

it was dark before
        i'd even half begun.

back home safe,
i stare through the kitchen window.

there's mum,
at the table
on her own.
how easy to sneak up and frighten her –
to bang on the window,
and make her jump.

she sips tea,
dunks a biscuit,
checks her watch,
rubs her head and yawns
and then stares at nothing for a while.

why don't we go out together any more?
my mother does not leave the house at all.
she taught me all about her shame
and left me alone with mine.

her face lights up like Christmas
when i walk through the door.
i sit with mum.
we listen to the rain, and talk about
how today's not the day to be outside.
we watch TV.
she measures, pins, stitches, sews,
creates beauty for those
who already know how lovely they are.

talented,
my mother is.
she blushes if you say so.

she works with
silk and lace, velvet, net –
mysteries of grace
that drape the room
in dreamy folds.
she stitches
tight skirts

fitted to the skin.
things that i could never wear.
(would never wear
how they'd STARE.)
                  "let me make you something pretty."
mum pats my hand, holds out
a pattern.

i shake my head.

                  "so everything's all right, then?"
she asks,
biting off a thread.
i nod.
i try to tell her how
happy i am at school.
but the friends who every day
pretend to smile and
       then
       look away,
say that they will sit with you at lunch,
then
disappear,
pretend that their birthday didn't happen,
not that you weren't invited,

are lurking somewhere here,
present
in the calls that never come.
in the messages i don't receive.

i take a picture of my face and
wonder
is it good enough to share?

i know i take up too much room.
that there
is more fun without me.

i bring her lies from outside and

                              she serves up love
                              spoonfuls of kindness,
                              platefuls of hope
that make me choke.

and then, as if she knows,
sometimes she takes my hand and says,

                              "one more year, lil,
                              just one more year."
and i think about moving on
and leaving her behind.

planning who i might become
is something
we cannot resist.
except i don't think she realizes
i only want to get away
from this.

NEW SHOES

i've been ignoring all the talk,
cotton wool for ears,
but,
then,
at break on thursday, mollie says,
"you coming tomorrow? stacey's thing?"

the girls pull me over.
i know better than to
believe,
but they're smiling
and seem
so real,
hide my smile in my sleeve.

my friend,
(true friend?)
old friend,
(real friend?)
mollie.

our history began
with our first day at school.
finger-painting
playing house
daisy chains and hide and seek,
jumping in puddles,
secrets, stories, sleepovers at hers.
until just lately. not so much these days.
not really for a while.
so i'm a little shocked
to be included.

yes, *all right*, i say,
thinking fast,
regret already beating hard, making my blood rush,
cheeks flush.

i've got nothing to wear,
you know.

"well, don't worry."
she shrugs, "that's okay."

they slide their eyes
to one another
then to my feet —
share more than a glance.
"i've got these shoes,
don't need them any more,
you can buy them off me if you like,
thirty quid,
they'll look cool," mollie says.
(i don't miss the smirks. i'm not a fool.)

no point asking mum for
the cash —
dad's payday
is weeks away.

but i know where she keeps
her secret stash —
money she got when granddad died
and that she keeps
for
emergencies.

i'm thinking this counts.

FRIDAY

we catch the bus to hers.
mollie talks non-stop
about the boy she fancies,
how she plans
to get with him tonight
if things go right.

her mum sees me, exclaims in surprise,
"how are you, lily? it's been so long!"
we run upstairs,
away from questions,
we laugh and plan.
i watch mollie transform.
(but i'm not staring, just snatching a look
now and then
as i pick at the polish
that's already
peeling from my nails.)

her jeans are tight and ripped.
her top is short,
a second skin,
her breasts pushed up high
and her stomach taut,

still tanned from summer
(or bottles of sun —
orange,
fake beauty,
better than none).

she watches herself, pouts and preens
likes what she sees, turns to me.

now it's my
cue.
i can nod,
look up,
exist
for a moment,
now my opinion is
required.

"do i look all right?"
mollie already knows,
but, still,
i tell her she is beautiful.

"god, i look so fat,"
she says
still staring at

the girl in her mirror
who gleams –
resplendent
and
astonishing.

you look amazing,
i tell her again,
thinking about shrinking.

she doesn't thank me
and i accept
without complaint the fact that she
does not reciprocate.

LAST YEAR

mollie invited me round hers,
and i stayed the night.

on monday morning
she told them all

i'd watched her undress
and she'd caught me staring

pervy lez.

OUT OF THE DARK

they go to a party to dance,
i go
to watch.
to see how the business is done:
the work of growing up, of creating
yourself, the hatching and flourishing of
girls,
butterfly bright,
dragonfly gold.
(their teeth as sharp as fangs
their nails like claws.)

i sit at the edges.
the shoes
are too tight
to stand in,

don't fit me at all,
(i didn't say a word
handed over the money,
and something else
that made me burn).

stacey's house is transformed:
darkness flashes,
music pounds,
the air is full of smoke and lights.

the boys
huddle, shove.
the girls
scream and strut.

like venturing to the moon,
a group begins to dance.
they know the steps
synchronized,
jump
        ing
                back-
        wards,
                for-
                        wards

shoulders turning,
bodies sliding, quick, fast, streaks of brilliance, white
teeth, bright eyes.

so much skin.

i stare.
everyone understands the way they ought to
be.

(maybe
i know, too.
maybe
i have learned
upstairs in my room, quietly tried out
these steps.
imagined moving
lightly, easily,
made of air, everyone watching, seeing
at last, that i am just like them.
dreamed it, at least,
because
the mirror would have laughed
if i'd have let her see.
she would have reminded me
not to be
such a fool.)

RUN, RABBIT

the varnish picked clean away,
i chew my nails,
wonder, should i leave?

mollie dances towards me,
pulls my hands and drags me up and off my chair,
into the crush.

out of the edges, out of the darkness,
i totter centre stage
the beat thuds
i like the boom of it,
catch the rhythm,
move my feet and hands and arms,
begin to
twist and dance beside my friend —
next to her no one will notice me.

but kids from my year
circle near,
clapping, smiling,
jumping to the beat.
"go lily, go lily!"
what?

my skin prickles
i look for the door
mollie steps back, becomes the crowd, lost —
i can't catch her eye.

another face
aidan vaine.
he dances closer
so
i step away.
he shakes his head
and pulls me in.

panic
      heat
            spreading
                over
                      my
                cheeks
                    and
                        neck,
itchy
      and
            red
                panic

crawling
    up
        and
            over
                my
                    chest.

"come on, let's see you dance,"
he says,
and —
      when nothing happens —
except that he just nods
and smiles — a smile that is not a smile,
      a smile that threatens more than it could say —
i hesitate,
then
decide

okay.

what choice do i have?

aidan gets closer.
i've never liked him,
never, ever could.

but everyone is watching,
and everyone will see
that maybe it's okay
to like a girl like me.

aidan plays football,
thinks he's a man.

he's all mouth and muscles,
there's stubble on his chin.

everyone hears about the girls
he says he's had.
and the things he's done on a friday night
drunk
and
high.

time i
sidle off,
sit down,
safe,
because right now
vertigo strikes —
        i wobble,
                almost fall

but he isn't letting go.

he's closer still,
his breath on my cheek
sour, not sweet —
warning signs.
he smells of drink.

i lean away from the scratch of his skin
   the thickness of his face,
     and heavy breath.
       but he's moving nearer, stretching towards me,
                towering over me.
it is the first time a boy has
touched me like this,
been so close.

well.

(unless you count that time
last year
another party here,
they're all watching porn.
her brother
pushing your hand
into his pants.

you freeze.
you
do not know
if you have the right
to **scream**.)

backing away
i think i'm smiling,
even as my heart hammers
because
he'll feel the sweat on my skin,
the bulges at my waist,
he will know,
if he touches me
everything i hide.
(he knows already,
fool —
didn't he hurt you
on your way home
from school?)

i force myself to last
another second
and another.

look into darkness and it stares right back —

with an eye that
blazes,
angry and alive.

aidan's arms are tighter, he's welded to me now,
as the beat explodes,
and i'm crushed into his bones
the music
rises,
             it's pulsing, pounding,
                         juttering and demanding,
and aidan has me around my waist.
he's shouting like he's having fun,

                               a whoop!
                               another!
faces leer,
fists punch the air, as they close in
on him
on us.
hands and hips and mouths,
making gestures,
                  something foul,
                              obscene.

      something i wish i hadn't seen.

and aidan's laughing,
        then whispering in my ear.

what is it?
he's still holding on.

what? I say.
lean back, away.
he laughs.

he smells of dead things
of the alley near our house
of the leaves
and the gutter
and i can smell my own fear –
its stink on my skin.

   he's swinging

             me

  round and round

        "Yee Ha!" he cries,
    "Yee Ha!"
and i shrug and struggle,
     but i cannot throw him off,

he's got my clothes, my flesh
my body in his hands
             and he's pulling and grabbing, riding me –

on my back,   so heavy he's crushing me,
             bucking
     and squeezing
             buttons popping
     my brain exploding
             no one hears me
     or knows i'm screaming.

"Yee Ha!"

                              he hollers,
     as he spins,
             and my
feet are tangling, my clothes are tearing,
     ripping, in tatters,
i grab at my top,
     try to hide my breasts, my flesh

but
he won't let go.
they're roaring, jeering,
bent double, laughing –

and aidan holds on.

how long is it before i get away?
i shake.
face burning
throat raw
eyes streaming.

everyone saw.

i stumble somehow out of there
force my way free.

mollie's disappeared,
but,
i hear her laugh
and crow,
"did you see the state of her?
those shoes!
can you believe she thought
that we actually wanted her here?"

outside autumn's arms are thin and cold.

WHAT

did i ever do
to aidan vaine?

there's nothing to say,
no way to explain

why he hates me
because i simply exist.

maybe he hates me
because i don't resist.

HOW TO HIDE

"what happened?" mum asks,
she's breathing, fast and heavy,
face flushed,
hot and bothered,
panting panic,
taking all the air.

i push her away –
there's too much that
i can't say.

i'm fine,
i tell her
she stares at me,
blinks,
worried eyes,
creased with questions,
and the hallway
waits for all the words
i'm keeping under lock and key.

i want to ask my mother, who decided
that girls who look like me are wrong?

who says girls like me are not allowed to dance
or run or swim and know
that they are lovely too?

the mirror laughs
i told you so.

i want to smash its smirking grin.

you should go out,
i shout at mum.
stop being so pathetic. get a life.
although i really think that everyone
should be allowed to hide.

because if you were to come and force her
out of this hole, like a fox beaten
into the chase of hounds, i wouldn't think
that fair, or right.
i say the words
harsher still,

it's your fault, mum,

i hate your guts,

and leave her alone to cry.

BEACH

here's a memory.
years ago, but sharp.
my mother sitting
far from me,
as if we're strangers after all.

who cares about the beach, the sun, the sky?
i can only watch her sitting there,
alone,
as if she does not belong and has no right
to even that one square of sand.

come and play with me,
i call, as if
sandcastles and shells and ice cream cones
will be enough to make her smile. and yes,
she lifts her face,
but then she shakes her head, and seems
to draw a wall around herself,
a barrier i cannot break.

head in a magazine, she waits
until i've had enough.

it was supposed to be fun —
a holiday!
we were going away,
making lists of things to do,
dreaming of waves
and hot, bright days.
planning and packing, excitement growing —
sunflowers bursting bright yellow into
the grey.

clouds passed across the sun and i
wondered why she wouldn't feel the sea against her
skin,
the sun on her shoulders, the sand between her toes.

she sat apart from us as if she did not want to tar us
with the same brush,
she kept her body over there and for all she hid
everyone stared.

we are not beach people.
not summer people.
not shorts and t-shirts and strawberries and cream
on long green lawns with a view of the sea folks.

BERNADETTE (4)

Your daughter's eyes
Ash grey,
Burnt out.

You'd waited up,
Hoped she'd come home
Happy,
That tonight was going to be the start of something
Better –
Friends, at least.
But her face is white and
She won't meet your eye.

She holds her coat tight around herself, shoulders
hunched,
Her face downcast.

"What's wrong with her?"
Joe asks, home at last.
Face full of expectation,
Arms wide in unreturned affection
As she charges past him, up the stairs.
As if I ought to know.

Teenagers,
I say.
They're cruel.
Don't worry it's just a phase,
She's just a bit moody these days.

And there is nothing I can do.

SCREW SCHOOL (2)

i don't want to go to school.
no one likes monday.
it's drizzling
and it's grey
and
i
feel
broken.

i stand beside the road

it's
early and dark,
and
easy to cry here
in the cold
with no one else around.

traffic pounds.
i stand and wonder
if i dare step out
when the next truck thunders hugely by.

i see the tarmac open up
to swallow me,
and hate myself
for being too scared
to jump.

no one speaks to me all day,
but they're not afraid
to look and laugh.

i sit in class and try not to feel
the eyes on my back
the judgements made.

try not to hear the talk
What a laugh!
Did you see . . .
State!

i sit forward on my chair
try to shrink to fit
the space
not to spill over the edges
like too much custard
jelly
gravy

something thick,
disgusting.

i get out of my seat
stumble over
a chair leg,
tangle myself up in my bag,

whistles
hoots
jeers

aidan winks,
rolls his tongue
around his mouth
grabs his crotch
thrusts,
stacey grabs his arm
and laughs.

SPEAK UP

miss stands at the front, to explain
the latest torture:
a speaking task,
she says,
"it's part of your GCSE –
think about your grades
your exams,
i need you to take it seriously."

i worry all week,
knees shaking
feet tapping
nail biting
heart racing.
talk about something that matters.
talk with passion, make a mark,
she said.

i want to tell her i can't do it,
to point out
how bad this will make me feel,
but i imagine her questions,
her disapproval,
her knowing exactly why.

so i spend hours in my room,
thinking, preparing, writing, practising.
if i say it well, perhaps the words
will do the work.
and they will not see
the rest of me.

i am going to talk about war.
about how one day i intend to leave
all this behind and find
the people who are really hurt.
how i intend to help
or heal.
i tell my mum over tea
she nods and smiles
and says,

                              "yes!
                              that's amazing, lil,
                              what a great idea!"

later i practise in the living room.
peering out from behind swathes of silk,
mum gives me a round of applause,
but it echoes hollow, bounces off walls,
and slaps me into wondering,
if anyone will hear my words.

STICKS AND STONES

miss calls me up,
summoning groans.
i hear those words again, on aidan's lips
pig girl!
fat slag!
yee ha!

i feel my face burn
and pluck at my clothes.

eyes swivel onto me,
faces that don't bother
to look as if they care.

can i even begin
to
speak
about
the bombed and the broken,
the decimated and the dying?
my
     voice

s

      h

        a

          k

            e

              s

hands too,
wordscomingoutfastandquiet
tripping
     and
         stuttering,
holdingcardsthatblurandsmudgeintoseasofnothing.

i know i believe
these words matter.

the classroom buzzes:
phones beep,
voices leap,
somebody snores, feigns sleep,
i can't compete.

but i talk and try
not to care. i try
not to notice the way they stare
at bits of me that are too **large** and
fill my clothes.

bulges, **fat**, no way
to pretend it is not there.
pretend not to hear the words coughed into fists,
or see the boys
on the back row.
aidan smirking.
mollie sneers.

i might as well
be naked, the way their eyes strip and weigh
measure, assess, take stock.
miss says *shhhh*
but no one is listening,
not to me and not to her.

i am no more than my size, and that size makes
me nothing and too much.
a
paradox.

MAY BREAK MY BONES

miss, please, can i sit down?
the teacher swallows.
nods.

BUT WORDS WILL NEVER HURT ME

stacey stands up.
the classroom stills.
they know
she will have something on her mind.

"right, stacey," says miss,
"do begin."
relieved – she knows this will be good:
the class will listen,
she will not have to try to make them shut up
and be still.

(miss is young, voice small,
mouthing nothings into the void.)

but
when stacey smiles and looks at me
i know
that this is something
that it may be hard to hear.

"disgust,"
she says,
then pauses.

(drama queen she loves this moment
flicks her hair, works the room.)
she shows the first image on the screen,
talking as if she is a pro.
a picture of an ostrich neck,
bloody,
plucked,
full of holes.

"trypophobia," she explains.
the class crane forward, fascinated by the sight,
twisting to see, to get a better view.
"it's just disgust," she says, and shrugs,
"at something gross.
it's normal, a natural, human response."

she shows us other things:
vomit.
shit.
she holds her nose,
the class recoil.
people pretend they're being sick.

i know what's coming, can feel it in my bones
by the way stacey pauses,
then looks at me,

as she clicks to her next slide.
she clears her throat,
begins,
"gro   sso   pho   bia," she says,
she spells it out,
le   tt   er   by   le   tt   er,
sou   nd   by   sou   nd
lingering over the long moan of an "o"
hissing out the "s"
rolling the word around her mouth
and then spitting it out.

she nods,
gestures, makes her point
at me, ever so subtly,
and says,
"it's an evolutionary thing, you know,
perfectly natural
to think,
**god, i'd rather die,
than look like that**."

she points again, this time
at the woman on the slide whose body
spills over a bed, whose eyes seem lost in
the flesh of her face.

"not only is this woman fat,"
says stacey,
(as if she is qualified in the subject,
has studied long and hard,
gained a PhD,
and now is gravely sure)
"but she's morbidly obese.
can't move, can't walk
just eats and eats and eats."
she raises her eyebrows, shakes her head.

another slide
piles of junk food
crisps and chips and sweets and cakes and bottles of
coke and takeaways
she flicks back to the woman
the classroom laughs
she stills them with a glance —

        "it's serious, guys,
        you know
        this is what we pay our taxes to support.
        she'll die an early death —
        self-inflicted —
        waste millions on the NHS."
        she shakes her head —
        "i call it greed."

she looks at me and smirks.

blood is throbbing in my ears
a pounding gun,
the room is spinning round and round
i sit there,
dumb with disbelief
horror firing up my face,
shooting helpless glances
at the floor.

(she's been to my house
just that once
in
year seven.
mum was kind
but i could tell
it didn't work
and stacey didn't eat her tea
and called her mum
to pick her up
early.)

miss says stacey can take questions.
hands punch the air.
stacey plays the room, smiling

laughing,
nodding along.
who's the fattest person you know?
can fat people have sex?
would you be friends with someone fat?
why are all these losers getting things free on the NHS?

later, mollie says
(her sympathetic smile,
a pose,
an act
      – pretending
      that she hasn't said
      things
      about me,
      behind my back)
that stacey didn't mean to be cruel.
"when you think about it, lil," she says,
standing next to me as we queue for maths,
where i can't get away,
the corridors a maze
that catch and hold and
trap me here,
"it's for your own good, you know,
we're just concerned about your health."

i want to tell her to go fuck herself.

IDLE TEARS

our house is small,
a box, lidded and sealed,
cramped and squashed too close
to too many other people,
not far from the busy main road
in a part of town no one wants to live in and
everyone wants to leave.

i wander outside,
look for a place
to wait the evening out
a place where i can breathe.

there is dog shit on the streets,
windows shuttered, boarded up,
cars that don't start,
broken things
lonely things.
people leave their trash
on street corners,
spilling out for
everyone to see.

"oi, lily," mrs burns yells from number 53 —
standing on the step in her nightie,

her dog in a pram beside her,
thin and old and finished,
"oi, girl, what you up to?"
i walk in the other direction,
head down, pretend i don't hear.

in the
precinct
by the
shops
you see
people
sitting
frozen
on
wet
pavements —
statues
numb
with the
drugs
they've
taken to
anaesthetize
their
pain —

half-
slumped
on
benches,
not even
half
alive,
soaked
through
to the
bone,
but
the
rain
doesn't
clean
anything
up,
it
just
        drops
and
        falls
so
        many
pointless
        tears.

FENCES MAKE GOOD NEIGHBOURS

our garden is a square,
a patch,
fences high enough to hold us in
and keep intruders out.

i end up back there,
sitting on the step,
watching the night close in,
as clouds bank up,
and a bitter moon swallows the streets
gulping down their pain,
greedy for the darkness.

dad put those fences up one summer,
labouring hours
in a vicious sun
and mum watched from indoors
waiting to feel safe again.

i run inside,
upstairs,
and lock my door.

i cover the mirror in my room,
hide from my shadow,
just in case
she sees me
and recoils.

i write their names
somewhere nobody will see –
the people who
make me fall, who push me down,
who laugh and sneer and mock

and store their faces
like a secret
to take out later
and destroy.

SPEECHLESS

later mum calls me down.
i stare at my plate. don't touch the food.

my mother wants
to know what's up
    — swipes at my tears,
        i leap back from her touch.
there are no words to say the things
i've heard and felt and seen.

i push back my chair, stand up, lurch away —
fight through
half-sewn dresses,
fancy gowns,
and party clothes,
pins and needles,
everywhere.

standing behind the bathroom door
i punch myself
stomach, thighs, face, arms
add new bruises,
make new marks.

this body that i cannot change
(although i've prayed,
so many times
to wake up
new)
right now, will pay.

i think about my mother,
hear her calling from downstairs,

>   "lily, please, come eat your tea
>   it's getting cold."

i think about the way she walks up and down this
house
each day, slowly, cleaning,
wearing out her slippers, breathing hard
but still moving, trying,
even if it hurts.

not gross
or a loser
not a failure
not someone to laugh at
or to despise.
just another person
doing the best she can.
(but why did she have to be my mother,
why can't she die?)

staring at the bathroom's sheen, the rows of neatly
folded towels
the polish on the shower tiles
i think about the smell of my clothes, washed and

clean
the perfect ironed creases in my father's jeans.

i think about how mum hides away and know
she isn't strong enough for them.
but strong enough to keep us whole,
she thinks, just by doing this.

how weak am i?

i walk downstairs.
stand before my mum and dad.
and tell them everything.

my mother's face dissolves,
my father roars.

i sit before them, trying not to feel
their pain on top of mine
staring at my hands,
hating that i've made them sad,
until dad says,
"i'll ring the school,
i'll go down there
let's hear the little bastards
say this stuff to me –

give me their names, lil,
we'll go round their house,
sort this lot out."

and then i have to beg.
no. forget it,
who cares? they're nothing,
dad, please, you can't.

"that's right," he tells me, "less than that.
you are better," he tells me, "in every way."
and his fist encloses my palm and holds it there – tight.

i wasn't always like this, lily,
i dream i hear mum say.
i dream again
see her stand up from the towel and run across the
beach
towards the sea, her skin bright white.
i see her dive beneath the water,
disappear for a second and then emerge
on wings.

BERNADETTE (5)

How can they be so cruel?
Joe doesn't answer me,
But I can see
He's simmering, boiling, ready to blow.
"Didn't you know?" he asks.
And I nod.
I knew.
I see it all,
All the invisible
Scars.
The marks
That living leaves behind.
The fingerprints,
Faded footprints
On paths she trod alone.
Ghost palm prints of
Hands that held hers
When I was not there.

Teeth marks.
Tiny incisions.
Pieces of her nibbled out of existence

By sharp words or faces.

Great chunks removed with a sneer.

How to shore up a body against the onslaught of
eyes?
Fool to think love is enough,
My child.

Did I make the world
This way?
Did I teach you to be afraid?

You'd think
Our skin
Would be
Thick enough
By now.

YOU GET KNOCKED DOWN?

"where's the fight in you?" dad says.
it's late.
he's come up to my room
(he never comes up to my room)
and is perched, awkward, on my bed,
elbows on his knees, hands clenched,
staring at me
with eyes that insist i listen.
i can see the rage in them
they fire at me,
strong words –
come on,
be brave!
and although everything in me wants to
look down
to crawl under my covers and
hide,
i nod, just a little.

"don't cry," he says,
"come on,"
he insists.
"where's my lil?
you want to change things?

well,
don't be a victim,
right?
you hear me?"

his hand on mine,
i stare at the tattoos on his arm
our names
inked there.

his words are hard,
but soft, i guess, for a man who works all day,
and then comes home to us
to face the facts
that we're not right.
probably not the family he dreamed of
loving
and being
proud to walk beside.

what am i supposed to do? i say.

dad doesn't mean to shout
when he tells me to fight back, and
i don't mean to cry.
maybe it is because he cares

and not many other people do.
"that's self-pity that is,"
dad says,
and he shakes his head.
"that'll get you nowhere fast."

i want to
scream at him,
you don't know what it's like,

i want to tell him that when you're in the gutter
you're litter,
     with the leaves that fall
        and the trash
            that's thrown
                out of car windows,
                    careless –

you're
crap.
down and out,
done.

but
he's up and off,
shrugging on his coat,
standing at my door.

"i'll be back later,"
he says.
"me and you,
we need a plan."

EXPLANATIONS

my aunty clare comes to visit with her kids,
mikey tears around our house while
my mum's sister sits outside and smokes.
her boyfriend's useless, and she's broke.

mum smiles and helps mikey to create more fun,
monsters out of empty boxes, string and glitter.
glue goes everywhere, he laughs
and daubs his painty fingers in her hair.

i watch them, amazed
that all it takes is
hearts that are not sour.

when i first started school
my mum went back to work.

she loved the little ones,
the busy, funny days.
the kids she cared for loved her back,
and cried sometimes
when their own parents came and pulled
them from her arms.
one day a woman came to look around
the nursery to see if it might be good enough
for her precious child.

mum gave the tour.
tried to chat and handed toys to the little boy,
showed him books,
explained the day.
said she understood how hard it was
to let them go, and walk away.

the woman looked at her and didn't smile.

         "she didn't like the look of me,"
my mother says.
         "i lost my job because of her.
         i should have had a thicker skin."

why? what do you mean? what did you do?
my mother waits

and then she says
in a voice that doesn't sound like her,

> "that woman called my boss.
> she said
> that she couldn't leave her child with
> me,
> she said
> that she did not believe that I could
> take care of him or
> do my job.
> not with me the way i am."

i still don't understand.

mum sighs.
her face is closed.
like this all hurts
too much to tell.
like she's sick of explaining herself away,
her words come out, slow and low.

> "she thought that i might
> influence him. that he might catch
> bad ways,"

mum says.

as if she is a germ.

as if she could infect that kid,
as if she could not be trusted to
take care of that child as if
he were her own.
she takes a breath.

        "too fat,
        that woman said I was,
        too fat
        to move.
        health and safety, my boss said."

mum shrugs.

        "maybe it's true."

she was a bitch,
a bully, that's discrimination.

        "that's the world we live in, love.
        so i was hurt.
        i came home.
        i shut my door,
        i thought about those words
        i tried to change.
        well, here i am.

        i'm sorry, love, i've let you down.
        it's all my fault.

i'm going to try from now on,
to be better,
get out
a bit more,

i've let this go on too long."

my fingers sink into my skin.
i'd tear that woman,
limb from limb.

stop it, mum. it wasn't you, i say,
and think about how cruel we are to one
another every day.

PART TWO

BOMB

the thing swings there in the twilight darkness.
dad slaps it with his outstretched fist.
huge and black and ominous,
it dances
daring me,
not to back away from this.

my hands are strapped,
confined inside the clumsy gloves,
stiff and snug,
hefty, hard to manage.
really? I ask
"yes," dad says, "why not? why shouldn't you?"
and so i do.

i swing.
first strike.
the bag waltzes out of reach and i sink
into the soft mat,
my legs leaden, slow.

how long we stand out there in the cold
getting warm.
how long dad patiently

explains that there is a technique
and if i want to learn, i'll have to try.

what's the point? i ask, panting and sore,
my arms aching with the effort of swinging
and punching again and again but failing
and glancing off into the air.
i won't be any good, i say and he
takes my face between his hands and stares at me.

"when you were born," dad says,
"i didn't know
that i could love another person quite
so much.
your granddad came to see you
and he took one look at your face and said –
she's a bloody little belter, joe.
so don't you ever tell me you're no good.
just give it a go, lil.
see that bag there,
imagine it's those girls.
      imagine their faces.
           imagine you're smashing them into pieces."

YOU GET UP AGAIN

i've spent years making peace and keeping it.
easier to swallow pain and smile
than to say,
No.
You're wrong.
No. You lie.

it's guts
i need. can i become the kind of girl
who feels
that winning is a right?

mum stands on the back step
in the darkness watching me.
if i can do it —
so might she.

all right, i tell my dad, *i'll try*.
"good," he says,
"one two.
like this."
he demonstrates, his own old gloves
fast but slow enough for me to see.
and something changes on his face.

intense,
      he thrusts again,
              hits harder,
shows me what i have to do.
then, pausing, smiles,
teacher, father,
as if there's no way i can lose.

"it's been years.
don't know why i stopped.
      your mum,
she didn't like it.
      — said she liked my brains right here,
inside my head."
      he taps his skull,
"but it feels good.
now you."

i don't look at dad as the punchbag swings
away from me again,
      mocking,

                  too swift

and   cunning

          to be
              caught.

i try again.

he's patient, waiting,
but everything depends on this.

i see their faces on that bag. their smiles.
their lying smiles.
stacey.
aidan.
mollie too.

my breathing's harsh, just standing here,
remembering.

they blur, dissolve,
eyes flashing, lashes sweeping over
cheeks that glow, long legs that run too fast
for me to chase and catch.
just one, then, pin her there, yes,
clear skin, dark hair, fake smile.
and her eyes
so wide
and cruel
looking at me for all these years,
then the whispers, flickering glances
that say it all.

i hit it hard. i think i scream.
dad laughs.
"that's it! again!"
and then the pummelling begins,
i'm swinging wildly,
madly,
crazy,
with all that i might do. holding the
bag, throwing myself at it,
battering the thing like i want it to break,
like i could knock the stuffing out.
and
for the first time
there's no pain.

HOW COME

they hate me?
what did i do?

questions roll around
behind my eyes
as i lie in bed,

trying to sleep
and i mutter my prayer

dear god
please let me wake up
someone new.

GET UP AND GO

doing this means
crawling out of bed
too early the next morning,
pulling on
a hoodie and sweatpants,
dragging myself
downstairs, aching already, from the backs
of my arms, to my shoulders, my thighs, my bum.
every bit of me
complaining.

dad is already dressed.
the lights are too bright.
i squint, gulp juice, feel old
before i've started.

"good, right then, let's go."
i pull on my trainers. at least it's dark outside.

dad hadn't realized i am so slow.

he's not much better.

"better give up the fags," he says
stopping to cough and hack
into the morning mist.

we move in the shadows,
street lamps flicker and buzz.
he stops.
          waits.
                    jogs beside me again,
doesn't say a thing. we make it round the estate.
i walk a bit, run a bit, try not to notice
him beside me, try not to think the things
he must be thinking.

i stop myself from saying
let's give up,
forget this.
forget me.

BERNADETTE (6)

Off they go.

My girl is strong.

I swallow,
Skin prickling
Pride and fear.

They disappear.

I pick up my mug
Sit in the dark,
Tea hot in my hands.

When she was small
My Lily wouldn't even hurt a fly,
Cradling spiders, ants, in her tiny hands
Rescuing bees from puddles,
Making homes for snails,
So soft.

And now

I have to watch her
Hammer out another way.

Joe's right, I suppose.
Something needs to change.

DAY ONE, DONE

"well done," dad says as i crawl back home.
the sun is coming up. it's too bright now.
i squint into the street,
search the windows, the road, for signs of life.
no one has seen us.
"same time, same place, tomorrow," he says,
his face is set.
he reaches out, puts an arm around me.
"proud of you," he tells me.
i pull back.
don't. i stink.

it feels good to wash it all away.

not so good to know that now there's school.
school happens whatever you do.
                    "just this year to go, love,"
mum says, handing me my bag.
                    "it'll pass. all this will pass."
i smile at her, nod.
i know. thanks, i say,
and wonder if
i'm too young to wish my life away.

NOISE

"it's not just violence," dad says to mum,
"it's about taking control.
handling things
that are hard to handle."
he slaps the table with his palm.

he doesn't sound like dad.
dad doesn't do feelings,
asks us how we are and only hears:
fine.
in fact, i thought he'd run a mile
from pain;
i've never seen him cry.

they're still at it.

he pulls the dress from mum's hands —
the rows of tiny pearls she's been sewing for weeks,
and
something tears
and
someone swears.

it is new, to hear them disagree.
like this.

                    "i don't want her thinking it's right,"
mum says,
                    "my daughter isn't one to fight —
                    she might get hurt."

dad speaks, too firm — it makes me flinch.
        "**our** daughter,
        is already
        hurt,
        bernie."

and then there's
quiet.

i should go in there, tell them to shut up,
that i don't need them talking
about me.
my dad goes on, insistent, strong.
"and she needs something.
otherwise those little sods, they'll just keep up with
this."

mum's voice rises,
the old refrain,

> "there's one more year. that's all.
> then she can move.
> a sixth form college. make new
> friends—"

dad interrupts.
"there'll be others, won't there, though?
no.
life's tough.
she needs to be strong,
to hold her own."

BERNADETTE (7)

I never promised to be
Beautiful.

You found me
That night in your local,
I was there with the old gang,
Who've vanished now,
Into lives where I'm not welcome,
But who I called my friends back then.
They were drunk
And dancing on the tables.
And I was the quiet one.

You bought me a drink,
And we talked.
I think you made me laugh.

Later,
You told me
You liked my eyes,
That you liked the way I cared
About everyone,

Even you,
Who no one had ever really loved before.
And I fell for you,
Because you were strong
And you made me feel
Chosen.

Your arms have always held me
When all the world is cruel.

You watch me from the door.
"It's three a.m, Bernie," you say,
"What the hell?"

The blue light from the fridge
Illuminates us.

Joe takes the plate out of my hands,
And empties it into the bin.

Inside I scream.

STILL FRIENDS

sometimes mollie acts like we're still friends
and i don't know how to tell her that we're not.

it's easy to see how i fit in –
stacey away on a trip,
sasha off sick,
or maybe they've fallen out
and
pushed mollie to the side.
then that's when
she comes to me –
but only if no one else can see.

i don't listen as she talks.

my thoughts are full of twilight darkness
the damp fresh air and leaves and rot
all the shadows of the world out there,
the lean-to with its hanging bomb.

"what's up?" she says,
"you're quiet – you're not still
going on about that thing with stacey?
can't you just get over it, i mean

yeah she can be a cow,
but seriously, lil,
grow up."

i open my text book, pretend to read
and curl my hands into aching fists.

NO EXCUSES

if someone sees me.

first the jogging, up and down the street,
slug slow
round and round the estate in the dark.

then,
every night, after dad gets home from work.

he buys a skipping rope and i laugh,
remember being small and rushing
out to play, getting in line to
jump and turn the rope, sing the rhymes.

it had taken me ages to get the hang of it,
but mum had stood outside with me
through those sunny hours,
turning the handle,
aunty clare
on the other end,
as i stumbled and tripped
until suddenly, i flew.

"too slow," dad says,
"you need to get your feet
moving, girl. give it here."
he demonstrates.
the rope tangles in his ankles.
"just like that,"
he says, looking up, giving me a wink.

but i know what he means. it's all about
speed.
moving so it almost doesn't look
like moving at all.
like dreaming of dancing and
spinning swift
as if you are truly free
(not here and heavy
weighted to the floor

with iron chains that bind you to someone else's truth
of what you are allowed to be).

if i can do that, and do it well, that would be something.

my cousin mikey has come to watch.
"go on," mikey says.
want a go? i ask.
he takes the rope, looks at it, tries.
you have to jump, i laugh. *come on.*
i'll show you.
and i start and i don't stop,
even though everything is
wobbling
       jiggling,
moving,
       my t-shirt riding up,
in a way i'd hate someone to see.
but today, who cares?
i manage twenty, then muck up.

"you're really good," mikey says,
i hand him the rope, and dad nods.
"it takes practice. but our lil's great, isn't she?
just you wait, she'll be a star. go on try, mike.

now, lily." he turns to me,
"press-ups, right?"
a training plan is nailed to the wall.
i nearly say
No.
there are things i don't want to do.

"it's for your own good."
those words
make me want to scream —
can't he see that i'm trying?

the best time is hitting the bag.
not the squats or the kicks, or the lunges or the jogging,
out of breath, beetroot faced,
messy, jelly-legged —
but the confrontation
in that
imagined fight —
when i'm winning,
me against
the world.

"keep your focus," dad says,
"you'll be all right
toughen up, girl.

don't make excuses."
and i know there's no quitting.

EVERYBODY CAN CHANGE

dad used to bring home
bags of chips
and takeaway pizza

bars of chocolate
sweets,
our favourites, he said.

we'd sit
he'd drink his beer
and mum and i would eat our treats.

now, when he gets back
from all those miles
he's driven, all those dreams of home,

he holds out DVDs
Rocky, I, II, III, IV

Raging Bull, Million Dollar Baby.

and i sit through hours
with him
cheering on
heroes
who can rise
above the odds.

we punch at shadows together
and i start to imagine
those heroes could be me.

JAWS

mum sends me to the shops
for bits i forgot to buy last time.

i walk with mikey to the Spar,
pockets rattling, heavy with coppers and change.
we wander, wonder
what's to rush home for?
although out here,

in the evening gloom,
i'm not so sure
we're safe.

stick to the main road, mum said,
and i take my cousin's hand.

we talk nonsense,
laugh
at jokes he's heard,
and then
mikey says,
"do you think you'll be a star?
uncle joe says there's girls,
girls like you
who win big prizes,
you could get a medal," he says,
looking up at me as if i'm already gold.

"i'll come and cheer!" he jumps and laughs,
wafer thin, like aunty clare, a leaf blown on the wind.
not fair.
thanks mike, i say, although i cannot smile —
that wouldn't happen,
not to me.

"but you can try, at least, can't you?"

i s'pose, i say, it's worth a go.

(relax your hands, soft hands,
strong wrists — get the right technique,
keep moving, lil —
alone that night, later on
i'll hit the bag, one two, one two.
my arms like sponge, my head in bits.)

at school today
no one talked to me again.

and then,
at lunch, someone
caught me —
i felt the flash —
looked up,
into the camera's eye,
aidan and his mates nearby
and stacey with her girls.

i pushed my plate away,
too late —
the damage done.

so now there i am
all over their screens,
mouth open
fork raised.
minger,
fat cow.
pig,
      whale,
                so frigging gross —
why don't you just kill yourself?

"lily," says my cousin
as we approach the shops,
"who's that boy? over there?"
i don't need to look
to know.

gripping mikey's hand tighter,
i pull him with me.
he's no one,
come on
hurry up —
but i never have been fast enough.

aidan's coming over the road,
dodging cars

side-stepping through traffic,
upon us
smiling,
shark.

shit, i think,
and then,
he   s   p   i   t   s —
it hits
bullseye.

the traffic drowns what he says next
and i rake my sleeve over my face,
try to wipe him
off my skin,
but it's sinking in,

and his mouth
is open wide
ready to swallow me
whole
as it curves around
all the things he's going to do
as soon as he
gets me
alone.

in here, i say
pulling mike inside a shop,
wishing i could call for help,
but dad's away,
aunty clare's at work
and mum's no use.

we hide amongst the bottles,
amber, red and gold,
the guy behind the till
stares our way,
he won't want to get involved.

aidan is hanging at the door.
biding his time –
no hurry –
"what's happening? lily, let's go home," mikey whines,
shhh, i say,
just let me think.

there's only uncle ray.

AIDAN

both our dads went to Iraq.

aidan's dad never came back.

RESCUE

i call mum,
tell her to call ray
and ask him to come pick us up.

                              "what?"

and i have to make her understand
get uncle ray. i'm scared.

we wait.
i pretend to shop,
look for something to buy.
a can of coke is over a quid —
too much.
i close the chiller
and look again,
feign nonchalance

while sweat runs down my neck and spine
and my heart pants in wheezing time.

aidan's spit
is in my hair,
it's in my pores
and under my skin.

the bell on the shop door chimes,
aidan's inside,
walking up to the counter,
buying cigarettes.
he watches me,
lights up,
and blows cancer in our direction,
his fist curls around the smoke,
his knuckles glitter
brassy
with rings
and he
ignores the voice telling him to
get out
no smoking.
he's a lout.

("move. footwork," dad says,

"you can't stand still.
lily, come on, keep moving all the time.
if you keep moving, then it's harder to
hit you.
you need to move it, girl.")

aidan swears,
his mouth full of hate –
"you," he says, "dog,"
and our eyes lock,
"outside, come on,"
he cocks his head at the door,
"what are you waiting for?
let's go for a walk."

what would happen
out there?
the night is crawling
across the sky,
and in that monstrous dark
where people disappear
i'm sweating fear,
and aidan is destroying me.

mikey starts to cry
and there is no way

to get away.

the door pings again.
ray.

all shoulders and swagger,
in his uniform,
"everything all right,
lil, what's the problem, eh?
what's going on,
what you done?"

aidan backs down, slopes off,
trailing smoke behind him,
shoots me one last look
that says,
this will keep.

FEET UNDER THE TABLE

i have to be grateful now.

                              "show your uncle ray
                              what you've been up to, love,"
says mum, who
is serving beer and stuff she keeps
for dad, his favourite snacks,
and ray is filling his face.
now it's up to me to show how thankful i am, too.

mum looks as if she might disintegrate
crumble like pastry
like a slice of stale cake,
if i can't be strong right now
and take him away.

he grins at the punchbag,
grabs it, holds it fast.

"show us what you've got then, lil."
he watches, with folded arms
as i pull on the gloves
demonstrate my
weakness,

swiping
at my enemies
arms melting
legs shaking
belly a puddle of curdled milk.

ray laughs and
pulls on dad's gloves.

"you're going to have to do better
than that.
come on, hit me, make it hard."

he dances in front of me –
ducking
weaving
mocking,
beckoning me on,
and i try to catch him –
but i'm just so tired
of trying,
and even though i hate him
it's not enough.

"come on, fatty
come on, loser

come on, big girl,
catch me if you can."

ray's a big man.
and when he belts me
on the side of my head
i'm down
and i don't get up.

BERNADETTE (8)

The bastard.

Get out, I tell him
And I mean it.

He laughs in my face.
"Come on, Bern,
It was just a tap.
The girl's got to learn."

No, she doesn't,
I say.

And I tell my brother
To stay away.

SECRETS

                    "don't tell your dad, love,"
is what mum said,
                    "it was an accident, wasn't it?
                    he's never known his strength."
and my black eye is just
another bruise.

dad doesn't look convinced,
he's no fool.
"was it someone at school?"
i shake my head and follow him outside
to work my way out of this.

but i'm still no good.
not a natural,
no born fighter.

i hear the desperation in his voice,
see the tiredness in his eyes
and know i'm not living up
to what he thought he could make of me.
i pause, drop my arms.

i need a break.

"five minutes," he says,
cautious,
warning.

i step away, take off the gloves,
hand them back.

no, i'm done. i've got work to do. exams. no lie.

"all right. tomorrow, then,"
he pauses, frowns –
"unless you're backing out?"

i shrug.
am i?
maybe.
what is the point,
in trying to be something
you are not?

DINNER

my mother doesn't eat with us.
so much normal

so much strange.
but she cooks for us,
out of the freezer stuff.
or beans,
pasta,
whatever's in the cupboard
nothing special —
what we can afford.

but now it's protein, veggies,
recipes she's looked up online,
healthy eating
because, she says, i'm working hard, and
need my strength.

                        "you're an athlete now,"
she says, serving me
as if i don't have legs of my own.
i have to smile back at her.
i chew on the word.
athlete.
it doesn't fit.
er, not really, mum, i tell her
and push the meat around my plate
leaking blood making me sick.

mum shakes her head,
piles my plate higher.

                "you will be –
                your dad says you have good aim."
she mimes a punch.

dad laughs.
"she'll do well. i have a feeling,
lily, about you. you're just like your dad.
and your mum – she's strong, too."
a look passes between them,
then they're both watching me.
mum nods, welling up again.

she watches us eat.
have some, mum, i say,
wishing i hadn't the second the words are out of my
mouth.
the table goes quiet,
i start to fill the silence,
talking too much,
trying to make her see that i don't want to hurt her
again,
that i'm just trying to tell her that she is allowed.
we are all allowed to eat, for god's sake,
aren't we?

i mean, it's really good.
honestly.
i didn't say that to upset you, i wasn't trying to be a cow.

                              "i'm not really hungry, love,"
she answers,
reaching out to cover my hand,
                              "but i'll have some now.
                              that's a good idea, lily, thanks."

i jump up, get her a plate, and we all pretend not to
watch
her serving herself,
lifting the fork to her mouth,
pretend not to see
that her hand is shaking,
that her cheeks are on fire,
the most embarrassed she's ever been.

BERNADETTE (9)

I know
Size matters.
I have been big
And sort of small-
Er.
Not ever small enough.
Chubby as a kid.
Chunky
Then stocky
Then thick
Then big.
Big Bernie
Big Bird.
Then overweight –
Plus-size
Outsize
Obese.
Morbidly so, I'm told.

Hating my body
Every step of the way.
Fleshy,

Flabby,
Fat.

One thing I could have lived without –
And wish I hadn't listened to,
(They've taught me absolutely nothing new)
– Is all those voices that think they know my truth.

And although
I'm not allowed to argue
With their logic –
That I will die an early
Death,
Go heavily to my grave –

The funny thing is:

It's not as if they care.

I am simply someone else to hate.

IT GOES ON

it feels as if the walls will split apart,
like something is finally cracking,
smashing,
breaking up.

whatever it was that's been waiting –
laughing through the bricks
its breath stinking up the rooms –
is here tonight,
rubbing its hands,
nodding its head.

"you do this,
bernie, i'll leave you,
i swear,"
dad says.

                              "you wouldn't, joe,"
she pleads.

i don't know what this means.

and i cover my ears,
stuff them with pillow,
bury myself in hot silence.

does dad hate mum?
what have i done?

they go quiet.
i hear the shuffle of slippers on the stairs and
through the crack in my door
see mum,
a ghost, slipping silently downstairs.

PHYSICAL HUMILIATION

i've promised dad that i will not back down
or run away,
or fade.

i find a place to change.
pull on my tracksuit.
the t-shirt,
trainers,
bend to tie them tight,
hear laughter,
jerk up,
red-faced —

certain that it's aimed at me.
phones out
they look away.
i know what's happened
know one day i'll make them pay.

"running today, lily?" miss scott asks and i nod.
she raises an eyebrow, and that says it all.

i struggle at the back,
but don't give up,
each stride hurts
a bit more than the first
as i push myself on.
my chest burns
my heart hammers
breakfast churns.

miss scott nods and smiles
even though i come in almost last,
panting,
gasping,
loser red,
she pats my back.
"all right?"
i gasp out a yes.

walk past the others,
don't meet their eyes.

"fuck, look at the state of that,"
someone says.

BERNADETTE (10)

All it takes is a phone call.
I'd like to see the doctor, please.

The receptionist, suspicious,
Supercilious,
Already unhelpful.

Can she guess at my problem
From just the sound of my voice?
Do I give myself away,
My weakness?
Excess?
"What's the name?
Address?
What is it that you need?"

Here goes, last chance for me
To dive at my future,
Before it
Becomes the past.
I want my present –
A place where
Each bit of me deserves to be.

Will the doctor come out? I ask,

Another pause,

"I'm sorry?"

Home visit, I say, my voice quieter,

Hopeful

      Doubtful

                Why?

Why shouldn't I ask?

Add it to the list of things I don't deserve.

Time and respect,

Holidays and health,

Pleasure and prettiness.

A job.

Food.

Love.

She books the appointment,

The doctor's busy of course,

And I don't have the right to ask

Her to come here –

"It's no longer good practice," she says.

And my heart speeds up

At the thought of having to

Leave

The house.

I don't have a car.

Get the bus?
Walk?
It's too far.

Still, I set the date.

I don't tell Joe.
Not that night, lying in bed,
Not the next day, either,
That I need him to help me.
I've already tried
To explain.

IMPOSSIBLE

i'm asking myself what makes a woman.
a girl.
a female human being.

do i have to be fragile?
pretty?
silent?
do i have to sit back and let them laugh?

or

can i be strong and bold?
can i live like i want to?
smart and sassy,
spinning straw into gold.

it isn't easy to step out of the past and into now,
it's easier to hear all the voices that tell me

no.

i sit at the computer,
after school
the place deserted,

blinds drawn against the night
i search and search again.

Google throws up photographs –
boxers
girls, but not like me.
they have muscles,
bodies toned and hard,
they are fierce and fearless, full of fight.

i stare,
eyes lasering the screen.
searching for someone else.
not these women,
my impossibility.

i won't wear clothes that show my stomach
or arms
or short shorts
that show my thighs.
nothing that clings
or reveals
or would make someone notice
i'm here.

and i almost shut it down,

almost throw the monitor at the wall,
shatter the dream which is actually
just more
of a whisper
of a different life,
a shimmering
possibility –
out of reach,
glinting in the distance.

dad's dream –
his plan, is it mine?

ON FRIDAY NIGHT

dad takes me to the gym.
i tell him i don't want to go,
he doesn't seem to hear,
it's not what i expected, though.

no machines
on which people
with already perfect bodies glide

and sneer
and stare,
but a boxing gym
that smells of effort
and struggle
and might,
of sweat
and blood
and
fight.

"it's a new thing,"
dad says,
"lottery funds, something like that,
good right?"

no one really notices me.
no one cares.
too busy moving in their own worlds,
muscles shining
and pounding,
bodies working and hurting.

i wear a tracksuit,
trainers.
new things, too,

and i feel bad,
it's stuff we can't afford
for something i don't know if i can do.

i pull at the t-shirt,
look neither here nor there —
not one of them, for sure.

"need to get you some proper boots," dad says
looking at my feet,
then my face.
his smile drops, eyes question.
"what's the matter?
you okay?"
i just shake my head.
"all right, let's just watch," he says.

i'd been afraid he'd push me forward
into the ring.
that i'd stand there,
facing some girl i knew i couldn't beat,
a girl with wings in her feet,

that she'd smash me down
with one fast fist
and they'd all laugh

and finally he'd get it.

we watch together.
meet the woman who runs the place.
jane is blonde and bubbly
tanned and fit,
she grins and shakes my hand.
"lily, is it? great we're always looking for
new girls,
fresh talent."
i'm glowing red
with the embarrassment.
she asks me if i fancy a trial.
dad signs me up.
i look around again,
breathe out the fear.

maybe i can do it.

at least, i have to try.

TRICK

hallowe'en.
the nights are blacker still,
the clocks have changed
and i am chasing life
faster and faster every day
around corners and along streets
that are always different in the dark.

dad's away.
we don't put out a pumpkin,
never have.
mum doesn't need to explain.

instead we bob for apples,
tell spooky stories.
i paint my little cousin's face –
turn him into a lion, a clown, a vampire.
he tries the same on me and mum and aunty clare.
we sit patient, laughing
chew candy
our faces rioting colour.

the baby sleeps,
clare drinks wine

mum sighs,
happy sort of
and smiles when she looks at me.

then
there's banging on the window.
we jump,
mum screams.

it's all right, mum, just trick or treat.

the baby wakes and starts to cry.
                              "put out the lights,"
mum whispers,
                              "come on, lily, quick, hide –
                              hide!"
and i dive for the switch
as something else vibrates
against the glass,
(i knew they'd get in one day
this is no surprise)
mikey's crying, mum's face is pale.

it's up to me to put up my fists
and shout,
go away.

bangers explode
through the letter box,
eggs smash
on my face and clothes
as i open the door and yell into the night,
aunty clare swears and screams at them to leave us
alone.

mirrors glitter,
all over the house i hear them cracking
into laughter,
splintering
into sharp hysterical shards.

next time, i'll be ready.

BERNADETTE (11)

I have always felt
Empty

And Joe can't understand,
Although he should,
Because he knows
What it's like
To grow
Without
Food.

Joe, I say, *please,*
Come with me
Don't make me go alone.

"I love you as you are," he says.

But love,
Don't you see,
It's not about you,
I'm doing this for me.

HARDER

there are the beginnings of muscles beneath my skin.
not so breathless running any more —
head down, battering through
corridors
i make my way
towards the end of every day.

i just want to be at home.

the night sky **booms**
and glitters with explosions.
we stare together,
my family,
our faces tilted towards the sky,
the dogs of the street
wild with misery
howling their objections
in a chorus of complaint.

"first fight soon?"
dad wonders
and i pretend not to hear
but the swoop in my stomach
sends me running inside.

CATCH UP

every night after school
i train
teeth grinding up the excuses,
i think about everything
i can gain
and how doing this
means ending pain.

i get home, worn out,
nodding off over my homework
my head on the kitchen table.

                    "lil, are you alright?"

fine, mum, i mumble.

                    "you know you don't have to do this
                    if it's not your thing."

i want to, i say.

because this time i'm going to be the girl
who didn't fail.
i'm through with watching myself lose.

every day ahead of me, someone else,

another lil,
is running,
and she's holding her gloves high,
whooping and cheering
and she's free,
and she's alive
she's on fire.

i need to catch her.

THE REALITY

it's hard work.
jane doesn't make allowances
she expects me to keep up.

instead of running away
i hit harder.

instead of hiding
i pant and struggle.

hot and red and wet with sweat,

i try not to look at the other girls
who are happy to notice
that i'm not a threat.

BELIEVE

what do you believe in?
someone asks,
some teacher, speaker,
someone making demands
that we know ourselves, so soon.

i believe

a hall,
walls,
sitting in rows
like we're children –

i'm not sure i know what any of it means.

do i believe that
this is all there is?

blank faces
jaws chewing thoughts
of home,
even the teachers yawn
and check their watches,

believe in yourselves! the speaker shouts
and clichés tumble from her lips
like snowflakes —
melting
before they catch and stick.

whatever i believe in,
it isn't this.
marking time
until real life begins.

just leave me to be
let me become
my own sort of
someone.

SOMETHING BLOOMS

but then there's rosie
and i can't help but stare
at her face.

in the hustle of the gym,
she walks like
there are no clouds,
and if some should dare to appear
she'd just leap up there
and push them around
until the sky is only blue.

that face
with its smile,
that i'm hoping
i'll catch
and keep
with her friendship –
pocket it,
lock it
up safe,
is the shape of a heart.
she has
chocolate eyes

and soft skin,
rosy cheeks.
and the way she looks at me
as she holds the bag
and i punch
makes me sometimes forget
my own name.

my partner,
rosie,
who calls goodbye
and walks away
with a spring in her stride.

i'm glad
we don't get in the ring.
"not yet,"
jane says,
"you get out what you put in."
she means work harder
don't give up,
teaches me how to wrap my hands
watches as i lift the weights
and punch my arms out straight,
twist at the waist.

"you're strong," she says,
"but footwork –
watch the mirror."
(i look everywhere but
at the girl who's waiting for me
who looks like me
but who isn't me.
and jane sighs
and i see
the questions in her eyes.)

weight on your back foot
baby steps,
be ready to push
to throw your weight
behind your punch

her voice follows me
around school,
as i walk home,
and i try.

BERNADETTE (12)

Clare says she'll take me,
The baby bawling in the back.
"Come on!" she says
"Or you'll be late!"

I get my bag and keys and stand
On the front step.
The path to the gate has never been longer –
How long has it been?
Years,
I think,
I've been standing here
Weighing up
My life.

It takes for ever
But then
I struggle into the seat, with the belt,
Leave it in the end,
And my sister pretends not to notice.
"I think you're doing the right thing," she says.

People look up as I walk in,
And I have to pretend to smile.
Easier to look as if you do not understand
Why their eyes
Come out on stalks,
To act as if
You are not a sideshow,
A circus act.
Try not to let them hear you breathe.

I think I might just go home.
Don't think this can be done.

The doctor listens to my
Silence
Before she listens to my heart.
She is waiting for me to explain
What I want from her,
Why I'm taking up her time.
And I can't find my
First line.

READY?

she knocks me down –
holds out her hand
and pulls me up.

we try again.
she knocks me down,
holds out her hand.

i hold on,
perhaps too long.
she pulls me up.

"not bad,"
she says,
and i see her smile

as she knocks me down
and pulls me up.

"you've got to try
at least,"
laughs rosie.

jane is watching.

"come on, girls, let's move."
and rosie grins again,

lifts her glove to her head
pushes sweat from her face.
"this time don't let me win,"
she says.

and

so,

      i
give
      it
all
      i've
got.

rosie ducks.

she knocks me down —
and pulls me up.

NORMAL

"pizza," rosie says, drying her hair
staring in the mirror
and i wonder what she sees
when she looks there.

no one would dare
to mess with rosie.

"you wanna come?"
i turn my back,
struggle into clean clothes.
"a group of us are going,
it'll be fun?"

when we get to the place
people

smile.

and it's a shock,
because i'm waiting for them to do that thing —
sneers and sniggers, snide smirks that trigger
my desire to hide.

because i'm watching their reactions
as i lift the food into my mouth
the looks that say:
pig

(just leaves and greens, but still, i can smell
the pepperoni, and my mouth waters,
and i
would
kill
for a slice.)

"here," rosie says,
"take some."
as she helps herself to a mouthful from my plate.

no,
i shake my head,
and sip water instead.

because i'm waiting for the chair to break
for the girls to laugh and run away.

but
           nothing happens.
no one even looks my way.

rosie shrugs,
"aren't you starving?"
i'm on a diet,
i say out of the corner of my mouth, so the others
don't hear –
like it's a confession,
like i'm asking someone to forgive me –
her,
especially.

she rolls her eyes –

"eat the frigging pizza,"
she says
and puts it on my plate.
"it's good! and you're fine, lil,
i swear!"

BERNADETTE (13)

Blood pressure
BMI
Inches
Stones
Pounds
Kilos
Grams
Heart Rate
Pulse
Waist and Thighs.
Numbers which
Are all too high.

Highest marks I've ever had,
I joke,
But this isn't funny,
The doctor frowns
Reminding me that
I am indeed a fool.

She takes my blood pressure.
The first time a stranger has touched me in years,

And I don't look at my body
In her manicured hands,
But my blood races and pounds
I can hear it,
Rushing
Plummeting
Waterfalls of fear.

Scales next.
I shake my head.

All of me is trembling now.
She doesn't need to read a number to know the
situation.
The walls I've built around my life
Are crashing to the ground
Bricks and stones and rocks are flying, glass is shat-
tering
Everything is being stripped away
Leaving me exposed.
"There's no judgement," the doctor says,
But I don't believe her.
And feel I should apologize.

Instead I tell her what I want.

Dr Grice tells me,
In a voice that's stern,
That surgery's no magic wand.
It's a big decision.
To put your heart under such pressure,
It's no simple solution,
And there are risks involved.
There will have to be further
Consultations
And there are other ways,
You know.

Does she think I haven't tried?

Help me, please, I say.

And she looks at me,
With eyes that show
She knows
I'm human after all
And nods,
Okay.

GO!

next session
rosie isn't there,
and i train with kezia
who is new too.

except kezia
is one of those girls
who looks like she was born
wearing trainers,

and who can't stand still.
whose body just knows
how to move
without

      s

            t

                u

m

     bl

        ing.

"come on,"
she says,
"it's not hard,"
and i throw my punch again.

she ducks
and dives
runs circles
around me
and
i realize
how patient rosie's been.
how maybe she feels sorry
for the loser
and laughs about me later,
will soon move on
when she gets bored.

i don't want her pity,

i don't want my own.

too late.

kezia walks away,
doesn't look back.

then, just as i'm about to slink off,
jane asks me to stay behind,
i wait for what it is that's on her mind.

"look," she starts, then sighs,
and i know she's going to tell me
i'm wasting my time.

"do you really want to be here, lil?
i see potential,
you're strong
you're bright.
but –
it's time to bring it,
if you want to fight.
i mean, it's no fun
to get knocked down
over and over and over,
right?"

she puts her arm around my shoulder,
leads me to the mirror,
holds my chin
in her fingers,

i shut my eyes.

"you have the right,"
she says,
"to win."

SO PROVE IT

jane's pushing me,
but i don't feel like
taking it today.

her face is set
like marble, carved
to show no sympathy.

it's pouring outside
and i'm dripping,
hot and sour, drenched vinegar by the sky,

i've walked here –
miles –
so now i just can't begin to try.

"don't sulk, lil, get ready, let's go,"
jane says, pulling on her own gloves,
so,   slowly   i   step   up,

and duck into the ring
already heavy with defeat,
bricks in my boots.

i guess this is a test,
got to prove
that i mean it

that i'm for real
that i want this,
no matter how crappy i feel.

the others gather
again.
the trainers, the girls,

would-be boxers —
seems people like
to watch me fail.

and
something
lodges
in my throat,

a desperate
swell
of words
that want to

splurge, that make me choke –

can't cough it up
can't spit it out
can't swear or shout.

we spar.
jane sets the pace,
too good,

she's fast
and strong –
relentless.

ten,
fifteen,
twenty
minutes
pass.

time
is
a weight,
swinging
around my neck,
a heavy bell
that never rings.

IT HURTS

let me stop.

i'm crying

panting

doubled over

wheezing

on the floor

heaving

like   i'm   going   to   throw   up.

please, i can't.

i look at jane, asking for help,
but she shakes her head,

"you can," jane says,
not one bit out of breath,
"get up,

come on,
let's go."

no.

my audience stirs,
and i will them gone,
almost lift my head to swear,
but then
something happens.
i hear it first
as if from miles away
a whisper, a murmur,

my name —

"Li   ly,"
it begins,
and then,
"Li   ly,"
again
and again
"Li   ly,
Li   ly,"

they roar.

and i peer up
through the mess of my tears,
but no one is laughing
or taking the piss,
faces intense
urging
stirring
telling me that i'm better than this —
pushing me up
with the power of their words
so
i crawl to my knees,
and
jane holds out her hand.

i stand
all by myself,
and fill up my lungs,
take another step forward, back into the pain.

PAIN

wrists sore
knuckles bloody,
shaking hands.
only the moon can see
me work myself
into a sweat,
collapse
and

start again.

BERNADETTE (14)

If you don't take care
Of things they spoil.

Milk left out in the warm
Will curdle.

Flies will colonize
Meat, bleeding on a plate in the sun.

Gardens left to grow wild
Will become nothing but weeds.

And bodies,
Unloved,

May, for all you know,
House hearts
That have dried
Like leaves on a plant

Unwatered.

COURAGE

white mornings,
the sky like broken glass
and i'm running in the dark
and wondering how long
my heart will last.

and then i remember
that i
will
not
give
up.

CHRISTMAS SHOPPING

i stay late
homework holding me back –
i've let things slip,
so it's dark
when i make my way out of school,
doors slamming behind me.

"stay safe," miss calls,
"take care, lily, is someone coming
to pick you up?"
i pretend not to hear.

the wind sneaks inside my clothes,
the cold weaves around my legs
mottling my thighs
pinching my toes.
my skirt is too short —
though mum's let it out as far as it will go —
everything has its limits,
and there's no money
to buy new things,
not right now
with Christmas round the corner.

i wander into town
to stare at the lights
and peer into the shops
full of stuff
that might make you happy.

even our town looks
better
at this time of year,

and i catch the sound
of Christmas songs
as doors open into other worlds.

heat
leaks out
and pulls me inside,
warm with thoughts of what i might find.

saved bus money buys
perfume for mum
that smells of roses
and the pink that she loves.

i get dad gloves
and remember
holding his hand
when i was small.

stuff to say thanks,
and sorry too,
for all
of this aggro,
this whole ugly mess
a daughter who couldn't stand up for herself.

it's late
when i take a shortcut
down the old railway track
towards home.
there's no one else about
as street lights fade behind me,
pitching me into the dark,
and i hum a song
about last Christmas.

but the shove in my back
knocks the tune from my head,
batters the wind out of my lungs,
it sends me down flat
and i don't even
have a second to scream
before
there's a boot in my
belly
a foot in my face.

my arms over my head,
i try to curl
into a ball, like a snail in its shell,
but they're fast
and i'm winded
and

b r e a k i n g u p a l l o v e r a g a i n
fucking fat lez bitch
someone says
and something,
piss,
d
     r
           i
                 p
                      s

onto my face.

BERNADETTE (15)

My daughter collapses
Face half pulp,
Covered in blood,
She crumples when I open the front door.
Blood in her hair
On the collar of her shirt
Smeared on her hands.
Her cheeks are dark with mud and bleeding still,
Her tights are ripped,
Knees grazed.
The imprint of someone's shoe on her face.
I scream for Joe.
Then swallow the fear, reach out,
Did they – I can't say it –
She shakes,
And begins to cry.

Her eye is swollen closed
Her mouth thick,
Smashed lip
Making it hard to speak
"Mum," I think she says
And I hold her.

EMERGENCY

dad calls ray,
i hear it from
what feels like
a thousand miles away.

mum bathes my face
and holds my hand
and wants to know
if anything is broken.

everything, i almost say.
but the breath has been knocked out of me
and words don't work anyway.

dad and ray are pulling on their coats.
smudged shapes, they loom into the room,
"who was it?"
they demand.

and someone whispers,
Aidan Vaine.

A & E

aunty clare sits with me and holds my hand,
while a nurse patches up my face,
and checks i'm still alive.

apparently my heart is still beating.

although i feel
fairly finished, actually.

WHAT DID YOU DO TO AIDAN VAINE?

dad doesn't answer.
so i say it again,
dad, what happened?
and why'd you have to take ray?

"because he's a thug," dad says,
"they both are. him and ray."
it hurts my sides to laugh.
dad's mouth twitches,
then he takes my hand

and i wish i never had to let go.
"we warned him off, that's all,
he won't be coming after you now,
should have done it months ago."

i don't tell him i wanted to get him myself
and that next time,
i'll be ready.

EVERYTHING STOPS

for Christmas
and i wish the holiday would go on for ever.
after the slow, indoor days,
when we don't leave the house,
punctuated only by
presents and telly,
chocolate and board games,
late nights
and lie-ins —
i'll be back at school.

my bruises are green and purple, orange
and black and brown,
my face is a canvas
painted with someone's hate.

i talk to rosie —
we message each other into the night,
but i miss hearing her voice
and feeling her laugh
in the flesh.
miss her brown eyes
the way she looks at me
and seems to see
something different
to the things the world would like me to believe
i am.

mum's perfume smashed,
lost somewhere,
(i scrabbled for the pieces
in the dark
but it was gone)
so i've nothing to give.

ray passes me an envelope
when he comes for lunch

on Christmas day.
mum smiles and nods, and ray shrugs,
looks shiftily down at his dinner.
i suppose this is his apology.

when no one's looking
i sneak the money
back into mum's purse.
a debt i've left it late to pay
for stupid shoes,
when i thought that i should buy my way
into a world of people that i hate.

my parents watch me
with terrified eyes.

dad says next time he'll kill them.

YOU CAN'T HIDE FOR EVER

when rosie invites me to hers
on new year's eve —
a party!
i almost say no —
because — what if?

                              "what if what?"
                              mum demands.

i clarify,
speaking slow and loud
not bottling things up like before,
but letting them spill
                    like oil
a viscous mess
        all over her nice clean carpets.

what if her friends don't like me?
what if she doesn't mean it?
is only being polite?
what if?
        what if?
            what if?

mum fights back,

won't let me speak,

"don't be ridiculous,
rosie's your friend.
she wouldn't have invited you
if she didn't want you there."

i shrug.

mum shouts,

and it's
a shock

like the slam of a door on my fingers.

"you can't give up, lily,
you've got to at least try
not everyone's bad.
and
there's more to life
than feeling sorry for yourself."

HA!
i laugh in her face.

*says **you**!*
i mock
you've got no right to have a go at me,
mum,

when you're a bloody joke.

we're both silent then,
and whatever i've said,
i didn't mean
and can't take back.
still, i know it wasn't right.

BERNADETTE (16)

It hurts to send her out —
But if she stays inside,
For how long might she want
To stay in here and
Hide?

PRETTY

even though my face
is all made up,
you can still see
that somebody came after me.
nothing can hide
the fact
that i'm
the punchbag.

it's too late to run away,
and i pull a face at the mirror,
don't wait around for its reply.

"you look lovely, love,"

mum says.

how can she be so nice to me
when i've been so mean?

dad takes me round to rosie's —
we catch one bus
and another.
he wants me to be safe, he says,
as if i'm just a baby,
who can't go out alone,
but i'm glad of him

beside me.

rosie wears glitter on her face
and her brown skin
is smooth
and velvet.
how does she glow like that?
does she eat sun for breakfast?
swallow moonshine for dessert?

she takes my hand,
waves at my dad,
pulls me inside.
i hold on
and don't want to let go.

her house is big
the street posher than mine,
tidy,
the gardens firing light.
and rosie sparkles too —
she shines
sequined and bright
in party clothes
that i didn't know she owned.

"oh wow, lily,"
she says, taking me in,
"you look great."
i blush
look down,
at my jeans
and plain black top,
long cardigan,
still covering up.

she peers closer, frowning a bit,
"but what happened to your face?"

i choose not to say,
laugh and mutter about an argument,
and then there's no more time to waste,
she's introducing me to her friends
who smile and offer me a drink, a snack, a seat,
ask questions about my life
and listen when i speak.

"so you're lil!"
a smiley girl says,
"rosie talks about you all the time!"
and i blink
and swallow

and make myself
believe it's true.

there is beer
and wine,
someone has vodka
and rosie has made punch —
i've never seen her drunk,
she's loud, and wild,

big laugh, white teeth, wide smile, cherry lips,
her curves shout "look at me!" —
i watch
how she carries herself like a queen —
certain of her right to be seen.

grime banging through the speakers,
then hip-hop,
old school —
"mama said knock you out," they chant
and they dance,
a blur of feet, arms, legs and hands,
fast, on the beat, popping,
bodies rocking.

i watch,
remembering, and trying not to remember.

at first i'm awkward
don't know how to move,
but then the beat takes over,
i tap my foot,
feel it punching in my bones.

rosie's arms are in the air
and she's up in my face
rapping along,
Damn!
not one of the kids
from school
compares.

someone looks outside
and spots snowflakes falling
so we rush and
dance into the flurry,
it sticks in our hair,
we catch it on our lips
and count in the new year that way.

i didn't know
this happened
in real life.

PART THREE

AND I GET UP AGAIN

when i'm strong
and fast
and hard
i will select the thing
for its weight,
for the heft
and strike.
i stare at all the stuff
dad keeps at the back of the shed
the lines of tools,
sharp and blunt —
weapons.

i will walk along these streets
and lie in wait
near the school.
and when i see them
i will inflict
all the pain i've ever felt.

it will hurt them.

and i won't care.

reaching out i lift
an axe.
it drags on my arm
pulls me
low and slow.
dropping it, i walk away
feeling sick
at the thought of
all the blood i could spill.

JANUARY BLUES

back
to school,
to training hard
fight night waits, somewhere soon.

snowballs fly through the
dark morning
and something gets me
on the back of my head,
something
sharper than snow,

letting me know
it isn't over.

it definitely isn't over.

i walk away
through the whirling, churning storm.
ice in my hair,
blood,
on my hands,
in my thoughts.

aidan laughs at me from across the room
although he's wearing bruises, a black eye,
he knows that dad and ray
can't be with me every day,
can't watch me every second,
and aidan vaine thinks
he's going to get me again.

i stare him down,
then shut my eyes,
see the gym, rosie,
other places, better worlds,
starlit lives.

(but i also see myself
flickering,
brewing
waiting,
growing,
almost, nearly ready.)

at break i message rosie:
wish you were here
although i've never told her
quite how bad it gets,
i guess she's guessed
because, otherwise, surely there'd be friends.

people steer clear
but walking to maths
mollie is in my way.
"oh," she says,
"erm,
all right?"
          i shrug
                    what does she expect me to say?

RESOLUTIONS

repeat after me.

i am going to be the girl
who rises up
out of the mud
out of the gutter
out of silence
out of a void that has been carved for me,
an absence of destiny.

i have taken my rage
and i am eating it,
i am making something of it,
a self
that sings
a tune,
that one day everyone will hear.

there is revolution in me:
a great rushing thing
that drags me forward,
and i like the way it sweeps me up,
a tide,
a surge of blood,

that pulses with intent.

i am going to be the girl
who rises up
out of the mud
out of the gutter
out of silence
out of a void that has been carved for me,

i am a girl
i own my destiny.

READY OR NOT

jane says,
she's planning
who'll fight who.

it's time
to put us on the map,
she says,
and to show the world
who we really are.

i turn away
because i don't like hitting
rosie
and i'm scared that's what
she's going to make me do.
i choke on my complaints.
jane doesn't do excuses
i know there'll be no special treatment.

"our boxing show —
we'll run it every year," she says,
"well, i want to," jane adds, "if i can —
you've worked hard, all of you,
there's not so many chances out there for girls,
we want to put this place on the map, right, lil?
why shouldn't we be noticed? you all deserve it, too."

yeah,
but, i'm not good enough yet.

"we'll see," jane says.

we do circuits
all evening
and by the end of it
i'm dying.

"train," says jane,
and we train some more,
as if that is the only answer.

i message rosie
tell her what i'm thinking,
that i'd best pull out,
sack this off
while i can.

"don't you dare," she tells me,
calling up in outrage,
and there's no doubt
she means it.

i don't want to fight you.

there's a pause

another

"okaaaay," she says,
"well, yeah,
but everybody loses something sometimes,
babe."

but i lose
every single day.

those words stay
on the tip of my tongue
almost out there
but still not brave enough
to let her in.

"it's not the winning or the losing, though, lil,
it's the taking part,"
rosie says,
and then we laugh
and hang up.

AIDAN

looks at me
like he's won.

he has no idea.

mollie sidles up to me at lunch one day,
"hey," she says,
"you okay?"

i nod,
stuff my lunch
back inside my bag,
wonder what this is about.

"look," she says
her eyes flitting,
and i know that she's checking,
trying to make sure no one's watching her
fraternizing with the loser.

"i'm just worried –
it's aidan – well, you should watch out.
you called the police, right?
and told them he beat you up?

they warned him,
whatshisname,
your uncle ray, your dad,
they roughed him up —
maybe that wasn't such a great idea,
maybe you know, you should apologize?
just to clear the air?"

is this a joke?
i say,
and mollie
steps away,
holding up her hands.
"sorry i spoke,"
she mutters,
"suit yourself,
you freak."

OUT

she's always there
that's the thing
when i get home,
mum's waiting

but not today
the house is quiet,
no note, no message
as if it's conspired

to trick me,
send me running scared
into the street
as if i'd dare

shout her name
up and down the block
bang on doors
let them mock

didn't think she could walk, love,
i hear someone sneer
can't have gone far, love,
she'll be around here.

mum, i call, *mum* –
i'm a kid lost in the snow –
mum, where are you?
i don't want her to go

out of doors
the streets are sheet ice
the sky is like knives
the dangers are rife.

the doorbell chimes
mikey is here,
his friend's mum's dropping him back,
i pretend mum's near.

everything's quiet
but for my heart
missing its beats
on red alert.

BERNADETTE (17)

Bypasses
Bands
And
Sleeves.
The options
Go on for ever.
But the specialist says
I qualify –
My BMI
Is way too high.
In fact, he's quite surprised
I'm still alive.

No.
He didn't say that –
It was in his eyes.

"It's not a magic wand," he says.
"Your lifestyle, your diet, will have to change.
It's a long process,
You'll need to lose weight.
And, of course, there'll be a long wait."

How long? I ask.

Impatient at last,

I don't have time, I'm already almost too late.

BACK

where've you been?
i yell
are you okay?
mum looks upset
doesn't want to say
anything at all,
drops her coat in the hall
envelops mikey in a hug.

                    "i'm fine, don't fuss."

but where've you been?

                    "out," she says, "i got held up.
                    i'm back now, don't worry, love."

relief swells, but i'm angry –
she's acting strange
as if i'm stupid,
i know her ways –
this isn't mum.
fine, i say,
well, i'm off too.

                    "where?" she asks.
                    "training?"

too late
i'm gone.

SHOW OFF

i want to see how much i can lift.
pile on the weights
and push the questions high above me,
frustration powering my muscles,
pumping my arms.
i guess i'm stronger than i thought.
jane lifts an eyebrow,
slaps my hand —
high five —
and i
let a little swagger into my stride.

"but watch it, lil," jane says,
"don't make those arms
too heavy to lift:
light and fast, lil, light and fast."

no sign of rosie,
she isn't always here,
but kezia's in though.
"want to spar?"
i shrug and agree
it doesn't occur to me
to refuse.

we get in the ring
and that's when my stomach goes
and all i can hear
is my pulse
swelling in my ears.

i push in my mouthguard,
pull on my gloves –
look round
see jane at the ropes
a few others gathered.
what is this?

but there's no time to back out,
kezia's ready
grinning, waiting,
and fixing me with
her stare,
which means
come on!
hurry up!
too slow!

she gets the first touch
i forget to duck
of course it hurts,

i'm used to that
and let it slide
off me,
because there's no time
to think about how
sore you are,
how sore you're going to be,
no time to
plan or plot
no time to worry.

just move
      like jane taught you
like you've practised with rosie
      and dad
a hundred times
      a thousand.
gloves up in your bedroom
      throwing your punches
watching your feet
      moving through the days
like it's all been for this.

protect your face,
and find your space.

i get a hit
another
and again
it's kezia who's
caught off guard this time,
i take advantage
of my advantage,
of my size
and of my strength
suddenly feel
a thousand feet tall
when she's up against the ropes
breath coming fast
my feet moving faster
can't take it for granted
i'll win,
but i know i can try.
kezia fights back,
our fists start to fly.

how long has it been?
a blur of a fight
our four rounds are up
and no one is down.

she hits me again,

but my chin's granite now
though there's blood in my mouth –
i still don't fall.

jane steps into the ring,
"well done," she begins
and i like her smile,
wipe sweat out of my eyes,
as she starts telling us
where we went wrong.

i try to listen, and try to learn,
then finally, we're done –
i'm aching, burning, and tall.

kezia smiles
looks up, catches my eye,
"you got better," she says,
"nice one,
see you around."

FULL OF IT

i can't wait to tell dad,
but he's not there when i get home,
just mum.
it's so quiet
too quiet
not even the sound of her sewing machine,
or the TV chattering
in the darkness.

                                    "good time?"
                                    mum asks.

her face is pale,
her expression strange.
i say, *yes,*
i did well,
and wonder how much
she'd like to hear.
she doesn't really get it.
                        "that's great, love, come in and sit
                        down for a bit, i want to talk to you."
where's dad?
her eyes drift away.
                        "not here at the minute,
                        he'll be back in a bit."

something's wrong
and i don't want to hear it,
all the whispered anger
the heated exchanges
mum getting quieter, not speaking to dad —
dad going out, coming in late,
what's happened to them?
is he planning to leave?
but mum shakes her head,

                    "no,
                    he wouldn't do that
                    we're a team."
though her tears make me wonder.

so what's happening then?
might as well face it,
but there's no way i'm ready for
what comes next.

                    "today
                    when i was out
                    i was ..."
she swallows,
hands clenched,
like she's praying hard.

                    "up at the hospital
                    seeing a nurse,

getting some tests,
talking to doctors,
things like that."

and it all makes sense –
oh my god
are you ill?
oh mum,
what's wrong?
and i'm drowning in guilt for being a brat
i'm hugging her tight,
hating the fact
that i've shouted and yelled
been a spoilt kid
and she's got this going on
but all i've thought of is me.

"no!
hold on, lily,
that's not it.
please, i'm not really sick
or, i'm sorry,
i'm sorry, just listen
you've got the wrong end of
the stick."

and then she explains
what she's planning to do,
how dad isn't happy,
but he's just worried right now,
but she thinks that it's best
and hopes i'll agree
it will change her life
she wants to be

                                        free.

BERNADETTE (18)

The last thing I ever wanted
Was to let my daughter down.
Seems it's all I manage, though.
She looks at me
As if I've told her
I'm running away
And never coming back.

"But Mum," she says,
"You can't."

I have to.
I'm desperate.
I don't say that, of course
You can't tell your kid
You're no longer living,
Just waiting to die.

I know it's dangerous, Lil,
I tell her.
Of course there are risks.
Does she think I don't realize?

That I haven't been told?
But I've decided –
And yes, of course I'm scared,
I'm only human.
I tell her so,
And she runs from me,
Slams her door
Locks me out
And I wonder
If I'll ever do anything right again.

HARD

miss moves us around –
she thinks she can –
delighted with this,
her new seating plan.

is she insane
hasn't she seen?
the way that he taunts me
from across the room?

now aidan's beside me
my stomach sickens,
he sniggers and shouts
argues, won't listen.

he kicks his chair
then slumps down at last,
swearing under his breath
gestures at me, then the class

laughs along,
thinks he's funny
i shuffle away,
thinking of running.

then he reaches out
and lifts up my pen
chucks it to stacey
sniggers again.

stop it, i say
give my stuff back.
"fuck off," he says,
"you stupid fat slag."

he starts flinging my books
as the teacher protests,
laughs in her face
he knows she's no threat,

"pig girl," he says,
"come on, suck my dick."
shows me his crotch,
"you crap bitch,

fat girl wants it,"
he calls out to his mates.
my face is burning,
my body shakes.

get lost, i scream,

what's the matter with you?
but it's here, it's happening,
i know what to do.

he goes for my neck
tries to pull my head low,
wants to bury me there
wants to put on a show.

but i push and i shove
the desk topples, the chairs,
i use my shoulders, my feet,
as all my rage flares,

because this isn't happening –
not even once more –
i'm not a victim
time to even the score,

and

so,

i

swing and i **smash**

the whole room explodes
in shouts of delight,
nobody knows

who i am any more –
that i have a plan –
that i've played this one out
and won time and again.

"oh my god! look at her!
fight! go on! fight!"
aidan is coming for me,
won't let this lie.

his nose is bleeding,
still, he grabs and he lunges,
i duck and i dodge,
watch as he stumbles,

and because he's off guard
he doesn't know what to do,
he thinks he's too hard
doesn't know that i grew

harder than him,
wear a shell like a shield,

but he won't give in
he's not going to yield,

miss is crying and shrieking,
and trying to end
what is only beginning,
but if i want to send

them a message
that this stops now
i will have to go further
before i fall down.

jane's voice in my head –
that i'm worth something too,
dad's got my back,
and i swing through

with a hard left hook
follow through with a jab
he staggers backwards
didn't know i could stab.

my fists are on fire,
my monster is out,
he'll never dare touch me
not after this bout.

faster and faster
my fists start to bleed,
but i don't feel them hurting
he can't take my speed.

i'm only just starting,
want to go all the way,
want to make him see clearly
now i'm having my say,

but it's over so quickly
when someone catches my arm
and they're pulling me away
before i do harm.

it's what he deserves
why can't you see?
why shouldn't i fight back?
they won't let me be.

"for god's sake stop it!"
aidan's still on the floor
cradling his nose
but i want to do more —

blood will have blood,
isn't that the right line?
now it is true
this is my time.

i did it, i got him
and i could do it again.
i stand in the hallway,
feeling no shame.

PUNISHMENT

"this isn't a zoo," the head teacher says
"you can't just hit people
and think that's okay."

everyone is waiting for me to say sorry,
i shrug, shut my eyes.
i'm not even bothered.

"it's not like you," my form teacher pleads.
i don't care now –
i've seen him bleed.

it serves him right, i say in the end,
they aren't impressed
and so they suspend

me for a week.
i shrug

and say thanks.

HARDER

rosie laughs when i tell her about aidan,
and then forces her face straight,
wags her finger and says,
"don't tell jane."

why not?
she's the one who told me to
stand up for myself, i say,
pulling on my gloves.

"i don't reckon she meant like that,
i think she meant in the ring,"

rosie says, and **jabs** me
as we begin
sparring, panting, dancing
(at least that's the way rosie moves –
i could watch her all day
and all night).

"what did your mum say?"
she's not happy, i gasp,
as i duck, and swing,
but tough,

right?

in reality, mum cried
and dad swore.
but that had been about aidan really,
about the things he'd said
and which i'd written on a piece of paper
and pushed across the kitchen table,
unable to put
them into my mouth.

(i haven't told rosie what the fight was about –
if i say those things
then she might think them too,

234

might realize
that aidan's got it right.)

"good for you, lil," dad had said,
his face white
and pinched
as he tried to hold his anger in.
but mum had just wept, and wept and wept.
it made me want to hit her too.

ROCK

the only thing left to do is
fight
train
run.
work at getting harder,
faster.
work at not feeling
the blows,
at not feeling anything at all.

let them boo

or shout me down
laugh and look.
i can be stronger.
rock
that doesn't flinch.
stone
that won't cry.

don't want to be home
to see mum's face
her pleading eyes.
don't want to feel like telling her how hard
i've had to try.
that she's cheating
taking the easy way
risking everything.
don't want to have to bite my tongue and be
kind.

why do i have to be the one who understands?

OB_S__Y

am i stupid?
is this a test
to see if i can spell?

or, maybe you just like to be unkind.

i wanted to be a ballerina
like all the other little girls,
and to twirl
in acres of pink tulle
tutued up to the nines.

mum made my skirt
and i had ribbons,
long pink ribbons,
holding my pigtails high.
mum clapped as i danced around the living room
believing i could fly.

now i put on my gloves, and grit my teeth, and wait.

ROSIE

wants to know what's wrong.
nothing, I say
battering away
at the punchbag,
breathless,
not wanting to talk
to anyone any more.
leave me alone,
i tell her,
it's nothing.

"whatever," she says,
"but if you want to talk,
i'm here."

later i hate myself
for pushing her away.

sorry, i type
she sends back a smiley face and
hearts.

come and meet me
she writes
i'm bored, aren't you?

i sneak out –
that's what normal teenagers do –
and anyway,
i can't breathe here any more.

it's dark.
still only february,
the days too short
and the wind disgruntled, bitter –
snatching at my hair and clothes.

we meet in town
near the statue
that commemorates
the fallen.

i remember what i'd wanted to become,
not so long ago,
the soldiers i'd talked about
to a room of people who didn't give a damn,
people dying for their principles
for their country
(like lambs to the slaughter)
about
the horror
of war.

i tell rosie all about it.
how i hate arguments,
fighting,
conflict,
bloodshed.
how one day i want to be
someone who saves.

"oh, the irony," she says,
"remember, who showed kezia
a thing or two?
not to mention aidan vaine."

that's different, isn't it?
"yeah, of course,
i'm teasing, you idiot."
she takes my arm.

it's different touching her like this
even through the thick down of her jacket.
she's warm —
her hand,
no gloves,
squeezes mine.
"come on," she says and

pulls me through the streets
and

     somehow

           i

              keep

                     up.

we run nowhere,
     past the drunks in doorways
        and the lads out on the town
           the girls laughing in their stilettoes and
not much else.
     we run
        through the city,
          jump litter
            and the holes in the scarred streets
and i breathe it all in
     the neon blue night,
       the hell of it,
        the way it feels like
           we're going places
           and no one
              can stop us now.
don't feel the rain
biting my skin,

because i'm expanding,
     could swallow the city in one gulp,
          i'm flying
               floating,
                    airborne,
                         free.

"let's go back to yours,"
rosie says,
"it's nearer,
come on,
let's go."
breathless, flushed,
i shake my head.
no.
there's stuff
i'd rather rosie didn't know.

THIS ISN'T LIKE YOU

               "please talk to me," mum says,
               "we used to be so close
               you used to tell me
               everything."

what? ten years ago?
what does she know?
only what she wanted to believe,
that i was good and quiet and
not someone to make a fuss.
well,
actually,
not.

nice girl gets
nowhere fast.

seems like i'm someone else.
punching or running or lifting,
i push myself harder
and plan
to prove something.

press-ups,
squats,
skipping,
sweating,
i like the pain right now.

i work on my stamina,
footwork,

strength.
dad comes out to watch
and smoke,
it's the first time he's been home in days,
he narrows his eyes,
i can't tell if that means
he likes what he sees.

i hold out the gloves,
want to fight me,
dad?

he grinds the fag butt
into the ground,
pulls on his gloves.

"come on then, lil,
let's see what you've got."

we spar.

i hug him tight.
it feels good to hold someone –
even like this,
in a fight.

"all right,"
dad says to me,
"what's been going on, then?"

nothing.

"so why's your mum in bits, lily?"
dad says,
serious voice,
staring me down,
"this is your mum you're hurting.
sort yourself out."

RECKLESS

i hear them talking,
how aidan stole a car last night,
drove it round the estate
onto main roads
     drunk,

         too fast,

             he smashed it up,
wrapped it around a lamp post,

               and crawled away.

stacey's not in —
was she with him too?
their faces are scared,
and i don't ask
what's happened,
or why they care.

if i had a car
i'd drive
so far
from here
you wouldn't
even see my shadow.
aidan catches me staring,
and for a second our eyes lock.
i send him mouthfuls of hate
a faceful of disgust,
he swears,
gestures,
then someone pulls him back.

"so," mollie says,
coming over, eyes on her phone,
"what've you been doing?
you look good, you know."

a couple of other girls
join us at the desk,
like now i'm allowed in their club.

i shrug away questions
pull my coat around me tighter,
won't let them know
that now i'm a fighter

saving my fists
saving my words
saving my secrets
whatever they've heard.

"aidan's a wanker,"
mollie decides,
now she watches my face
as she pulls out the knives,
and shows me her phone,
"didn't you see?
stacey's a mess."

it's tempting
to chew it over with them,
to laugh on condition
i act like a friend.

i could speculate to
accumulate some
poisoned
ammunition.

save it for someone who cares, i say
and i stand up and walk away.

CONCENTRATE

in class i'm thinking
(as the teacher drones)
about footwork.

my hips
shifting —
left,
      right.
legs under my shoulders,
                    punching up —
feel my muscles
twitch and
tense —
i'm balancing,

        jabbing,

                sharp

                        and

                                fast.

outside, up in the sky, the sun is breaking through
and on the way home,
i see blue.

DRESS UP

at home in my room
i open my cupboards,
shake out the drawers,
pull clothes off hangers
and gather up the things
that were never really
me.

black bag full
i bundle it downstairs.

"what's this?"
mum asks.

rubbish,
stuff i don't need.

she's too slow to stop me
marching down the path,

i hear her calling though,
how i'm being silly,
telling me to stop
and sort through again,
together,
but

i drop it in a skip
outside number 38,
go home,
my arms empty,
head
full of possibility.

i need some money,
for clothes,
okay?

"how about i make you
something nice,"
mum suggests,

wiping her hands,
reaching for patterns —
i can already see pincushions of ideas
floating in her brain —
the lace, the silk, the miles of material
and her wrapping me up in it
rolling me round
trussing me up
swaddled and safe.

i shake my head
no thanks,
i say,
not my style.
i refuse to catch her eye.

"there isn't any money spare
this month, lil.
i'm sorry,
we're short right now."

when weren't we?

WINDOW SHOPPING

we meet in town.
rosie likes pretty things,
and
she poses
in dresses and skirts,
in short things,
tight things,
clingy things that show her curves,
and
floaty things,
long things –
she'll dress up in anything.
you'd look good in a paper bag.
rosie laughs – "why not?" she says,
and picks me out trousers,
patterned with stripes
others with checks,
a shirt that's cute
a jacket,
stylish stuff,
expensive
shoes.

"this would be cool on you," she says
and this, and this and this,
i blush as she oohs and aahs and i make myself
silly

      and strut,
laughing our heads off
    we dress up,
        and model for the mirror
           the camera makes it forever,
                blowing kisses and smiling —

we swipe through the pictures,
share one drink, two straws.

next to rosie
i like the way i look.

CHALLENGE

it's
just me this time
no other friends there,
and i don't dare ask if that means

rosie's picked me –
although i definitely feel chosen.

"come over,"
rosie said,
and now we lie together
on her bed,
watching films,
on her phone
heads close,
warm.

i like being in her room,
becoming part of it,
with the pictures of her, and her friends
her posters, jewellery,
flicking through her books,
searching for clues.

and then i blurt it out.

my mum's getting an operation, you know.

rosie looks stricken,
drops her phone,
grabs my hand,

"oh shit, why?
i didn't know she was sick,
are you okay?"

immediately i feel a fraud,
regret what i said
want to take it back.

no, yeah, i'm fine.
forget it, sorry, it's nothing, really.
"no, seriously, babe, you can talk to me."

i can't though. i gather my things
get ready to go.

"lil! wait! don't just walk out."
come with me then,
i challenge her,
come on.

TEST

it's not fair to do this —
to set rosie up to fail a test
she doesn't even know she's taking.

if rosie really likes me —
her face will give her away.
still,
i should warn her.

the kitchen lights are on,
we go round the back.
mum and dad sit at the table
playing cards,
laughing
at something.

i haven't seen them like this
in so long.

they don't stop when i come in,
but continue to smile,
and mum gets to her feet
and rosie steps forward
to say hello,

256

unwrapping her scarf,
taking off her coat,
like it's the most natural thing in the world,
for her to be here.

"so," rosie asks later,
as i walk her to the bus,
"what is it? with your mum? and you?"
nothing,
i say.

"sometimes you're weird,
lily, you know,
you've got to let her do
what she's got to do."

WHAT'S MY PROBLEM?

maybe i want a golden ticket too,
but for
me,
there's no easy fix.
i have to fight it out –

one on one –

play by the rules.

i cannot hit below the belt,
or bite or spit or kick.

can't hit when they're down.

or shrink to make myself fit.

anything else is cheating.

NEWS

we sit and stare
at the police in the corridor
someone shouts *pigs*
no one gives a damn about a uniform round here.

the head teacher comes in to our room
and looks around,
narrowed eyes,
face says: *we'll talk later.*

then,
he summons aidan vaine,

"step outside please, mr vaine,"

aidan's up
and swearing
throwing chairs,
tipping desks,
bull,
bully,
bulls-eye —

they've got him

and this time he can't run.

struggling,
but half-contained,
someone
takes aidan vaine
away.

i cheer.

(silently)

and
finally
i can
breathe.

THE INEVITABLE

"did you hear? did you hear?"
kezia runs over,
"we're doing it, it's real."
i know she means
jane's boxing show.

"it's all coming together, girls,"
jane talks, and smiles,
a blur of words
that get stuck in my ears:
charity, judges, referee, bouts
she's got it all sorted,
it's all worked out.

i start to walk away,
when jane calls after me,
"hey, lil. you'll fight rosie. you're up for it,
right?"

"when?" rosie says, already on her toes,
towing me with her
as i try to breathe
not to show
that this is the worse news i've ever heard.

THE MOMENT

fight night's
looming –
it feels
too soon.

and dad's been playing
Rocky music for weeks.
side-stepping round the house,
he's boxed and swooped –
making me laugh
and shake with fear
all at once.

i hide my head under my covers at night
at the thought of getting into the ring.

and so we train,
even harder than before,

every morning
before school
i run,
for ever it seems.

i think i'm even running in my dreams.

(running from
exams and
school
and
grades
and the fear that i won't get
even half of what i need
to build a future
that will see me
up and out of here.)

rosie doesn't seem to need to try.
everything comes so easy,
and even though
i can't hate her for that,
i don't like it when she swings
and
shouts
chicken
when i don't hit back.

"come on, lily,
chicken, licken," she calls,

darting ahead of me
        towards the main road
                like a kid, playing tag,
                        fooling around as if it doesn't matter.

hair still damp from the shower,
slicked back off my face,
clumsy in my joggers, backpack on my shoulders
i'm nobody's dream.
enough, i decide.
if she wants to be caught,
i'll catch.
we chase,

and then,

i stop her.

i hold on tight,
and we laugh,
her face is bright and smiling,
and her joy
is as delicious as anything,
so i catch it,
swallow it,
a spoonful of sweetness

that burns in my chest,
and right there
in the street
before i can wonder
what i'm doing,

i kiss her.

SHE LAUGHS

and i step away,
put my hand to my mouth
want to run.

"god, i wasn't expecting that,"
rosie says,
reaching out an arm.

but,
i step back again,
and try to gather myself.
i hear a hurry of sorries
spilling into the street

but don't hear
rosie speak,
although she keeps talking
her mouth moving, her words are far away.

i step back.
before she can tell me
that wasn't okay.

OH

"you want to come home with me?"
she says,
and i think i must have misheard,

shake my head, try to dislodge the glue in my ears.

she takes my hand,
the air crackles, electric around us –

and this time
i'm
the

one
being
kissed.

I'M WAKING UP

everything that's been asleep.

i don't know where to put my eyes,
my hands,
my mouth.

but rosie is sure enough
for both of us.

ANOTHER NIGHT

she takes off her clothes
and mine
and we lie
beside one another.

she takes my hand
and holds it.

she is soft
and i let myself touch her,
so, we lie like that

until

everything
is dark
and clear.

and in the morning
she's still there.

DON'T ANSWER

the world goes quiet.

if someone calls my name
i don't hear it,
if someone gives me grief —
whatever.

miss keeps me back at break,
"what's wrong, lily?"
i nearly laugh —
now, she notices.

i could make her a list,
but actually, all she's bothered about
is the homework i haven't done
(again).

"i'll have to ring home if this carries on,"
she says.
i shrug and walk away.
none of it matters.

there's just

rosie.

MESSAGE

I like to win you know
it says,

and then rosie sends
a smiley face,
blowing a kiss.

THIS IS ME, MAYBE

i've been thrown into space,
have landed on another planet
and i don't care if there's
no way back to earth.

i think
i'm finding my feet here
out in the atmosphere,
the pavements are clouds
and the sky burns,
ignited by the sun,
as hot blood licks
through my veins.

everything is
on fire,
and light
streams
into the far beyond.

i glow.

PUNCH DRUNK

what's happened?

that's mum.

lil, where's your head?

that's dad.

concentrate!

that's jane.

WAKE UP!

miss says.

but it's better here,
inside myself

working out
things
i never
thought i'd
need to understand.

MIRROR, MIRROR

i look at myself
and wonder what rosie sees.

i try to make my hair
sit flat
and straight.

i try to
like the shape of my face.

i try to
see myself

in a new light.

and maybe, in the corner of my eye
i catch a glimpse of
something special.

DON'T LET ME DOWN

but,
it's my fight,
i tell mum.
had i really been expecting her to come?

> "i'm sorry,
> she says,
> "i don't think i can bear
> to see you get hurt.
> i can't stand blood
> you know that, lil."

you've got to come,
why didn't you tell me before?

                              "i did,"
                              she says.

mum is hiding in her sewing room,
dad's waiting for me
downstairs.
if i'm late jane will go spare.
mum pins the material she's working on
and holds it up to the light,
not looking at me,
pretending
it's all right
for her to let me down.

i don't say again.
i don't say for the millionth time
i don't say
For All My Life.

                              "you don't really
                              want me
                              there,
                              and that's fine.
                              aunty clare will come.
                              and your uncle ray."

i pull a face.
great

"just you take care tonight,
that's all,
and do yourself proud."

(proud is what
i'd like
her to be.
of herself,
and me.)

BERNADETTE (19)

Here are the cupboards full of
Things you'll never wear.
Dreams you've stitched for yourself,
A rag doll happiness
That sits and waits behind these wooden doors.

You could sew something better.

Bernadette –
I see you
Bright
And
Fine –
In
Gold.

THE BIG FIGHT

i can't watch the others.
sit, head down, waiting,
nerves jangling,
legs shaking,
feel like something's
trapped
inside,

that monstrous pain,
that tide of rage.

i can't breathe.
i see rosie
inside my mind,
on the ropes, hurting.

i won't do it.

"lil, are you all right?"
jane waits for an answer
and silence bounces between us.

how can i tell her that it feels
like something's

already
over?

SOMEONE IS SCREAMING

my name.
it's dad and
aunty clare.
even ray.
their mouths
open and shut
but I don't hear the
cheers.

i'm wearing the shorts
mum sewed for me –
bright red.
like i'm a champ.

Lily Lionheart dad called me,
just joking around.

inside

i have my own roar
just

NO.

STRONG

where's the girl
i'm supposed to smash?

she's jumping,
nimble and fast,
feinting,
ready and
waiting.

we bump fists.

she's the girl i kissed last night
and the night before.

she told me i was pretty,
that she likes the way i smell,

and she likes the dimples in my cheeks when
i smile.

she's
smaller than me
but tough —
has muscles like rock,
and she likes to win.

i like that girl
more than i like myself.

but i could knock her down
with one hot blow.

because i'm stronger than her now.

IT'S TIME

to prove myself.

the gym flashes
and crashes with noise.
i taste sweat on my lip,
bitter and salty.
i'm standing in my corner
wanting to run.

rosie's opposite.
on the tips of her toes
bobbing up and down
ready
and bold
in blue.

i'm already sinking,
already done.

dad's waiting and watching,
the bell rings
he's cheering me
loud
his voice breaks through

fists pumping
shoulders twitching
egging me on.

>rosie's approaching,
>the look in her eye says
>*Come on, Lily*
>*You've got to TRY,*
>*Don't make this too easy*
>*Don't just let me win.*

>**Make me look good here.**

>she nods.

>we begin.

OFF GUARD

i'm watching for her right hand,

    she's circling,

waiting,

        but here come the jabs,

as she takes first swing

                      it's a glancing blow,

i move away

                        want her to know

that i won't fight back.

i don't want to lose her,
not over this.

                              i move

we spar

              the crowd is waiting

shouting,

                        i can't not start.

'cos when you're down
        you're a loser
                you're in the gutter
                you're done.
when you're down
        you're nothing
                you're finished
                they've won.

"LILY!"

dad's voice

that yell.

i look at him
his eyes are full,
he's waiting for me
to show them
what i can do.

he waves and points
and i see that
mum is here,
after all.
shouting for me.

and while i'm not looking,
rosie takes her chance.

oh.

i shake my head.
taste blood
pure and raw —
stagger
back
and
        find

                     my

                               feet —

duck
another
and then

it's time.

I

hold up my gloves
and
begin
to paint the ring with blood.

it's easy.

mum's wearing red
and orange
and pink
and the blur of her standing and cheering
for me
is all that i see.

it goes on.
like that.

a trumpet blast, a fanfare
lifts me –
i'm gonna fly now

simple –
as if i've always known
the steps of
this particular dance.

like i learned it
in years
of ducking
of waiting
of striking
out
at myself.

i know what i have to do.

to
batter
rosie
d
o
w
n

drop my hips.
breathe,
pivot,
force her back,
with a barrage of blows,

double-jab,

    right cross,

        roll under the left hook,

          follow up

            right cross

              left uppercut,

                right cross —

don't feel it if she hits me back.

i smother and fall
into rosie —
so she has to hold me up,

and then

she's on the ropes.

how many rounds?

it's done.

the bell rings.

and jane holds up my arm.

winner

i take off my gloves,
spit out blood,
and my mouthguard,
pull off my headguard,
and shake the sweat from my hair
let the cheers chill me.

gloves off,
am i still good enough?

BITTERSWEET

"you bloody little belter, lil,"
dad says,
he grabs me, spins me round, lifts me and whirls me,
in front of all those people,
in that ring.

"i knew you could,
i knew you would,
i'm so proud, girl!"

it's just one fight, dad, nothing much,
i say, and pull away and clamber down,
into the crowd.

my family are embarrassing.
ray's filling the place up with his gob,
"she's my niece, that's our lil,
she's a legend, did you see?"
i tell him to shut it,
but don't pull out of his hug.

                              "oh, lil," mum says,

waiting – right there.

                              "are you all right?"

she's crying,
but grinning
and she holds me tight,
i think maybe
her smile is worth
that fight.

THANK YOU

for coming, mum,
i manage to croak.

                                    she nods

and i wipe
the blood and sweat and tears away.

NO REPLY

rosie has her back to me.

when finally she turns
so i can see what i've done
i suck in my breath.

"congratulations, lil,
good fight,
i guess the best girl won."

her swollen eye is already glowing
with bruises

that i recognize – i've worn them too
and feel the throb and stab as if it is my own;
smashed nose,
the blood still smeared around her face,

but it's the look in her eyes that hurts the most.
i think i screwed up,
i think i really hurt her
in a way that wasn't right.

i didn't mean it,
is all i have the guts to say.

she shrugs, as if it's nothing, forces a smile
and i don't dare touch her,
as a million miles open up between us.
suddenly the world is very large
and i am very small.
it spins,
as rosie picks up her things,

this doesn't change things, does it?
i call,

and listen to her answer me,
by saying nothing
at all.

LEAVING

"are you going to prom?"
mollie asks
finding herself beside me.

word got round –
someone saw me
in the ring
and all the blood that
i left there,
rosie's blood,
which i never meant to spill,
follows me
wherever i go.

why would you care?

"i don't," she says, and turns away,
turns again, to face me –
"but aidan, right, you know,
he's not coming back."
and a small sort of smile
appears on her face.
"that's good right, lil?"

BERNADETTE (20)

Sweat.
Heat.
Swelling ankles
Fingers,
Rubbing thighs,
So much of me to disguise –
Breathless,
I cannot begin to summarize
The effort
Needed
To begin.

But –
I can,
I will –
I am.

When Lil goes to school
I take myself
To the local pool.

And there in the water
I float,
And swim.

EVEN IF YOU WIN, IT HURTS

i walk over to rosie's.
buy flowers from the garage, on the way,

a cheap bunch
cheap gesture,
scarlet petals scatter
and curl,
wilting in the heat
of my hand.
i throw them away.

she opens the door.
i step almost inside.
we face each other,
there
      on the step,

            deciding.

sorry, i say.
because someone has to speak.

"no," she shakes her head,
"i think i knew it would go that way,

you got good, lil,
better than me."
she swallows.
"well done."

so, you're okay?

"yeah, i'm fine. you know, GCSEs, all that stuff,
just busy."

i get the message.
i'm not stupid
and used to this.

but, it hurts —
            and pains holds
                    my heart in its clenched fist.

"lil," she calls after me,
once i've turned to go,
"look, you need to know,
that i'm not perfect.
no one is."

DON'T LET ANYBODY GET YOU DOWN

i miss the gym,
it's a funny feeling
but i've been itching to move.
sitting long hours
through exams that reach into forever
has made me stiff
and sore.
so,
i pack my bag
and open the door,
pull in a huge breath
just in case
rosie's there.

people call *hello*,
and jane comes over
to put her arm around me
and tell me she's glad
i'm back.

being missed feels good.
i work out at the bag,
and push myself
until i can only hear

my fists and heart
pummelling:
release.

it's only when i realize
that someone is standing near,
behind me, waiting, patient and still,
bronze and gold, her reflection
shimmering,
it's only when i realize who it is,
that i stop.
and turn around.

"lil," she says.
rosie shrugs —
the girls behind her
nod.
"good to see you, so,
listen, I mean,
come on, let's get out of here, let's go."

HOME

                                        "Summer's nearly here,"
Mum says.
I stop, stare,

Realize —
She's in the garden,
Hanging washing on the line.

Another ordinary, extraordinary thing.

                                        "Look at that sky,"
Mum says,
And she's right,
It's beautiful out here.

A butter sun slides off our skin
My legs and arms
Are warm, pinking in the heat.

                                      "I thought maybe you and me,
Could take a walk,
Round about,

Like when you were small,

                    Remember?
                    Our treasure hunts?"

She smiles, and waits for me to answer.

Okay.
And I have a glimpse
Of long-lost different days.

It's been ten years, I think,
Since
We've done this.

My steps match hers
We're slow,
But I don't care,

She talks as we walk,
Says she's got something to say,
And I hold my breath —

                    "Don't, Lil,
                    Don't frown,
                        It's good news,
                        All right?"

I breathe.

                              "Me and your dad,"
I suck my breath tight again,
She squeezes my hand,

                    "We talked,
                     He's right, I think,
                     There's lots of ways
                     To change your life—"
What? You mean, that operation?
I can barely speak,
You're not doing it after all?

                    "No, look, Lil,
                     I'm not sure, maybe
                     I will, I'm thinking –
                     It's hard, I need
                     The help you know.
                     Sometimes
                     You can't change
                     Everything on your
                     Own."
It's true.
I get it, and want to say,
That I'll help her, if she likes,
To find another way,

But I bite my tongue and listen
For a change.

>   "So,
>   I applied for a job,
>   Nothing much,
>   But I got it!
>   Can you believe that?"

I STARE at her, mouth open.

You what?

>   "Childminder,"
she says, cheeks pinking with pride,
>   "Taking care of a baby,
>   just the one.
>
>   The family are nice
>   They live round the
>   corner,
>   The money will help —
>
>   And I can still do my
>   sewing
>   In the evening
>   If I've any energy left."

She laughs.

I look at my mother
For what feels like the first time,

And I see her —
Underneath
All the pain she's been wearing,

Underneath
All the fear —
She's been there the whole time.

And I think
Of how
There's beauty

Everywhere.

I should have seen
Hers before.

PART FOUR

ROUND TWO

September again,
And Mum's right.
There can be
A start as fresh
As a clean sheet on my bed,
As a sun-framed morning,
And the bright green,
Of trees that still grow here
Despite the traffic and the noise
And the cracks
In the road
Out of which peeps
The stub of a flower
Bright and
Gold.

I make my way
Through wide open doors,
Into the noise
And chaos of another world.
But everyone else is new, too,
And so,
I square my shoulders
Standing tall,

And ready,
I smile
At strangers
And say, *hello.*

There's a flurry of footsteps
Rushing close behind,
Chasing to catch me –
And I turn as
Rosie steps up, breathless, and laughing
To walk there, at my side.

The bell rings
And it's time –

THE END

ACKNOWLEDGEMENTS

The hugest of thank yous to Bella Pearson, editor and publisher extraordinaire; thank you so much, Bella, for believing in this book and getting it out into the world. It is a privilege to be a Guppy author.

Many thanks to my agent Hilary Delamere at The Agency whose expertise and guidance have been a godsend. Thanks to Jessica Hare, too, for her support. Huge thanks to Ness Wood, Hannah Featherstone, Catherine Alport, Sam Webster and all at Team Guppy for their hard work and wonderfulness.

To my family (but especially my mum and Emily and Margy), and to Juliette – the best, best friend anyone could have – thanks for everything you all do to help me.

Thanks to the north-west SCBWI crit group for their invaluable encouragement, camaraderie and notes. Thanks to Sarah M-J who always boosts my confidence; Milene for creating my website and being such a staunch supporter; Alexia Casale for reading an early draft and generously giving brilliant advice and friendship, and lovely Amanda Jennings for being a fantastic help when I needed it. Thanks also to Teri Terry for your continued support and kindness.

A massive thank you to Lisa Williamson for the blurb.

To my esteemed colleagues at Loreto Grammar, Altrincham (especially the English department, un-paralleled in laughter), and to Jane Beever for being so kind: you are a marvellous bunch. A shout out to the fantastic girls I'm lucky to teach.

Thank you to all the readers, bloggers and librarians who make writing YA so rewarding and who have supported my writing so far.

Thank you to my dad, David Barry – who loved poetry, but who knows what he would have said about this . . .

And thank you to Alistair, Eve and Scarlett – you're amazing.